Descent

A collection of stories and poems

CW00383656

Descent

A collection of stories and poems

Descent: A Collection of Stories and Poems

A Bournemouth Writing Prize anthology

First published 2021 by Fresher Publishing

Fresher Publishing
Bournemouth University
Weymouth House
Fern Barrow
Poole
Dorset BH12 5BB

www.fresherpublishing.co.uk

email escattergood@bournemouth.ac.uk

Cover designed by: Kelsey C. Galpin

Produced by: Mariah Alexander, Kelsey C. Galpin & Luke Cole

descent

/dɪˈsɛnt/*noun*

1. the origin or background of a person in terms of family or nationality.
2. an act of moving downwards, dropping, or falling.

Foreword

Welcome to Descent, a collection of 25 short stories and poems depicting the highs and lows of being part of a family.

Discovering other people's stories is not only fascinating and compelling, it often holds up a mirror to our own experiences, helping us to better understand the people in our lives and maybe navigate our relationships with them.

Dip into Descent and you will find stories of both the bitter and the sweet side of family life, from losing a loved one to affairs and scandals.

All the short stories and poems you see here were entered into the Bournemouth Writing Prize 2021 which is run by Fresher Publishing at Bournemouth University. And this anthology was created by us, three students from BU studying MA Creative Writing and Publishing.

We sincerely hope that you will enjoy it.

Mariah, Kelsey and Luke (Editors)
www.fresherpublishing.co.uk

Contents

DNA

DNA

by Jess Fallon-Ford

You and I are so alike
It's as though we are one person.
One soul; in two bodies.
Afterall, the essence of her is in us.
From the day we were born
to the day we will die.

MY NAN

My Nan
by Les Clarke

My Nan always looked old. As frail and delicate as best
Sunday china, her hair a thinning clump of dry, lank
whiteness that revealed glimpses of pink scalp beneath.
Regardless of when we visited, be it summer or winter,
she always exuded the cloying smell of camphor. This was
overwhelmingly apparent in her dingy bedroom, where
should I be sent to get something, I would always have to
hold my breath or pinch my nostrils together to avoid the
smell or it would tend to make me feel sick.

Although Nan was elderly, somehow she never seemed
to get any older, but somehow remained constantly at the
same age. The only indication that she was ageing were
her slow and painful movements as she hobbled around
her cramped, tiny third floor flat. Sometimes she would
hang onto pieces of dark wooden furniture for support
whilst she paused momentarily to catch her breath. Her
twisted arthritic hands struggled to hold certain things and
bottles and jars became almost impossible for her to undo
or unscrew. Yet somehow she would always manage in her
own defiant well-rehearsed way, refusing offers of help with
a snappy,

"I can manage, I'm not an invalid, thank you!"

She doted on a moulting, overfed rotund blue budgie
called Peter that must have been almost as old as she was;
it had been her constant companion for as long as I could
remember. An omnipresent ear for a lonely old lady to
chat to and pass away the long daylight hours, until she
dragged an old tea towel across the top of his cage so he
could sleep undisturbed with the advent of night drawing
in. I recall on some visits, sitting cross-legged on the well-
worn rug in front of Nan's old armchair that had certainly

seen better days. If you turned your head to the side and looked underneath you could see springs and old horsehair stuffing touching the floor. I would sit there as patiently as I could whilst Nan wrapped skeins of wool around my outstretched arms whilst she repeatedly told me what a good boy I was and how she couldn't possibly do it without me. And after all my good work there was a reward of a rich tea biscuit to savour with a glass of orange juice.

On other occasions, I shelled peas from a rumpled brown paper bag into a pitted aluminium colander, sometimes joyously find slender green maggots that were afterwards washed unceremoniously down the chipped, tea and beetroot stained porcelain sink in the murky ill-lit cluttered lino-cracked scullery. I remember I used to fidget relentlessly whilst waiting anxiously for feeding time, when Nan would wrestle the paint-starved rickety wooden scullery window open and scrape breadcrumbs onto the flat roof below. Dozens of pigeons would huddle there, vying for position, and would coo their daily gratitude as they fought and bustled each other out of the way fighting for the titbits. Nan would smile and wipe her hands down the front of her faded floral-embroidered pinny and then wrestle the window closed again.

At afternoon tea I would watch and try to supress my giggles as Nan attempted to eat a biscuit. Her ill-fitting National Health teeth would move up and down in lop-sided fashion as she tried to chew. Then afterwards she would excuse herself and take a cotton hankie from her sleeve and turn to the side and she would remove her dentures and clean and lick off the crumbs and then discretely put her teeth back in with a pretend cough to cover her mouth as they clicked back in. When it was eventually time to leave, especially being a young boy, I reluctantly had to suffer the awkward slobbery whiskered kiss that habitually heralded our departure. It was sweetened and cushioned however in the firm knowledge that there was always a half-a-crown for me to collect from the tiled mantelpiece in the living room on the way out.

When Nan became ill, we never visited as a family again, instead my mum would take the train and stay for a few days leaving dad to look after us. When Nan died some few months later, we boys were considered too young to go to the funeral and instead were foisted onto a neighbour until our parents returned home late in the afternoon, looking red-eyed and exhausted. It wasn't until I was quite a lot older that I realised that Nan was really my mum's mum, and then I understood why she would go through bouts of depressed silence followed by secretive floods of tears. It's only when you're older that you begin to realise how much grief and suffering goes on all around you and how hard your parents work to protect you from the pain and the loss of loved ones for as long as they can, letting you just enjoy your childhood, until one day the protective parental mantle is dropped and you find yourself having to bear the unbearable and come to terms with death for yourself.

MY FATHER'S HANDS

My Father's Hands
by Alison Nuorto

My father was always ashamed of his hands.
Of those misshapen digits:
The result of a childhood accident.
Juvenile jibes made him self-conscious:
He dreaded handshakes and parties.
Nicotine smudges and brittle, bitten down nails,
Heightened their unloveliness.
In old age, his ill-fitting Wedding band, had to be wedged
on.
Those hands had endured too many winters.
His hands never could fill adult gloves.
Limply, the fingers would droop, resembling chickens.
As a child, I would trace the outline of his hands,
And run a finger along jagged nails, embedded in meaty
flesh.
As I got older, I resented how much my hands resembled
his.
Not quite a pianist's hands: octaves were a struggle.
Occasional remarks gave birth to my inheritance of shame.
But, as he lay on the sterilized sheet,
And the shrill beeping jabbed at my grief,
In filial observance, I placed my hands over his.
In wordless, inexhaustible grief.

CONTROL

Control

by Richard Hooton

I've known you for so long that I can't imagine life without you. It's as if you've always been there; a mysterious presence throughout the mists of time. I can't even remember when I first knew of your existence. You just crept into my life until there didn't seem to be a point when you weren't around, like a plant growing underground until erupting through to be noticed.

Mother, ever the avid gardener, would compare you to Leylandii, manageable to begin with before rising to overshadow everything else in the garden. You had more patience than anyone in my family. Your initial appearances were brief and infrequent, just waiting in the background until emerging ever more familiar. We became as close as childhood sweethearts and I presumed we'd be together forever. With that oh-so-useless benefit of hindsight, Mother tells me now how she could tell when you were looming, how she could see the changes, how much anxiety it provoked in her.

'I'd call you "the moods", Sarah,' she said. 'All those little battles. Stormy one minute, right as rain the next.'

In my teenage years I even thought we were cool, this romantic, brooding presence: Heathcliff and Cathy on the moors, Poldark and Demelza in the cornfield. Us against the world, stomping from dining table to bedroom retreat. In my head, we were the epitome of leather-clad rebels, burning with intelligence. With my pale skin, straw-like hair and crooked nose, I knew I wasn't pretty. Who would want a fragile, ugly creature like me?

'I'll never leave you.'

That voice, mellow as moonlight, before we disappeared under the duvet for days. As entwined as a married couple,

CONTROL

I was gripped. For better, for worse. It was while trying
to find my way in the world that you became difficult.
I couldn't get you out of my head. You made me think
differently, changed my viewpoint as easily as shifting the
face of a Rubik's Cube: a few calculated clicks and I was all
blue. You dripped a poisonous cocktail of self-pity, paranoia
and angst into my ear. The world was full of charlatans and
life was against me. You made me want to be apart from
other people.

'Ignore Jane,' you told me. She'd been my best friend
since school. 'She looks down on you, mocks you behind
your back.' I distanced myself from Jane, screened her
calls.

'Don't hang out with Andrew,' you ordered. I'd always
got on well with Andrew, since studying together. I really
liked him. 'He uses you, frequently cancels, never repays.' I
stayed away from Andrew, left his messages unanswered.

'Your mum belittles you.' There was truth wrapped in
the lies. Enough to cause doubt that rots into resentment.

'Pull away from her.'

My late teens were aimless, meandering, futile; mostly
spent holed up in a bedsit as if we were fugitives. By my 20s
you were an ice age dominating my world. I remember one
snowy Christmas, sat in Mother's kitchen looking out at her
beloved garden smothered in a white blanket. All life had
withered, bleached of colour.

'Everything's dead,' wailed Mother, her harsh grey bob
swaying as she viewed the scene with desolate eyes. 'My
sunflowers are gone.'

We both burst out in laughter at her melodrama. The
release felt like a thawing.

'It'll soon be spring.' She nodded wistfully. 'And then I
can get back out there again.'

Suddenly, without you there, I wanted more, wanted
better, wanted to connect. Life isn't staring at bare walls
between fighting you off. I'd been contemplating it, in
my good moments, I even still had the crumpled college

prospectus in my handbag. In a rare flash of decisiveness, I retrieved the brochure and pushed it across the table until it was under her nose.

'There's a hairdressing course I could try.'

She continued to stare at the icicles hanging from her frozen birdbath. 'If that's what you want.'

'It's something I've dreamt of doing.'

She blew on her tea, then sniffed. 'If you think you'll stick at it.'

I vowed there and then to qualify. Practically threw myself at it. I enjoyed learning a new discipline. Loved the softness and pliability of hair between my fingers and influencing its style. Christ, I even liked the responsibility of handling scissors! But you didn't want me to be free.

I'd grown two lives: with and without you. I needed people to see the upbeat, happier me, not the miserable version when you were there. With you around, people treated me differently; many kept their distance. I'd be flashed a sympathetic yet condescending look that said: "You sure you're all right?" I made excuses for you, pretended the problem was something else. Then, I tried to ignore you. That was when the real struggle began. No one likes rejection.

'You'll regret this.' That voice. 'You know what I'm capable of.'

How cancerous becomes a dictator clinging to power? You chipped away at my confidence, a sculptor hacking at their creation until nothing's left but dust. Worn out, unable to concentrate, my ambition was exhausted too. My attendance became so poor I had to quit. I shut myself away again, as if quarantined; didn't want to let you near other people, for them to associate you with me. Embarrassed and ashamed, I hid, like the mad, old woman in the attic, rejecting life. You had me all to yourself, this anchor chained to my ankle.

'Are you the devil?' I asked, the night I almost succumbed.

CONTROL

I'd thought that I was free of you that evening. Running a bath, I put my hand under the red tap's flow to feel the water's increasing warmth. Once it was full, I settled into the tub, trying to relax. Then you were there. Pushing me under. A riptide forcing me down. I held my breath, my only response little bubbles of air that floated to the surface. A reflex action kicked in. I struggled, pushed back, forced myself up, gasping for oxygen, arms flailing, water splashing over the rim. You'd let go. I clambered out of the bath, dripping all over the floor. I lay there, naked and gulping.

You spoke: 'You don't exist without me.'

I paced the bedsit through the twilight hours, drinking all I had, until the walls converged and I had to get out. Alcohol only numbs pain and fear until its foggy shield dissolves. At dawn, I found Mother on her knees on a small brown mat in her front garden, tending to her sunflowers. She acknowledged my presence with a little wave.

'You all right, dear?'

She squinted in my direction as if looking at a phantom. I didn't have the words. I think I nodded.

'Well you don't look it.'

Neither of us questioned what the other was doing, out and about at first light. We just stared at the sunflowers. Mother competes with herself each year to see how tall she can grow them. She set about spreading fertiliser on the soil around their thick, green stalks as I stood in the street and watched. Then she leant back to admire her handiwork. Bright, bold and majestic, they were already tall, with manes of golden petals surrounding black heads that reminded me of stereo speakers. Manure overwhelmed any sweet, subtle fragrance.

'They do cheer up the garden,' said Mother. 'And are so easy to look after – as carefree as their smiling faces suggest.'

The sunflowers are positioned by a fence and tethered loosely to stakes with a soft stretch of cloth to protect them from wind and rain. They're covered by netting.

'They're remarkably tough, will grow in any type of soil.' She tells me this every year. Without fail. 'They can tolerate droughts and take a chill or two.' I let out a weary sigh. 'But they still need a lot of attention. And obviously direct sunlight and regular watering.'

Mother climbed to her feet and we looked at the flowers with different expressions on our faces.

'Don't you ever miss Dad?'

She brushed dirt from her gardening gloves. 'There's no point in dwelling on something that happened so long ago.' Her gaze returned to her creation.

'No matter where you plant them,' she said, 'their faces follow the sunlight and absorb its powerful energy.' An idea struck me.

She took off the gloves. 'Would you like to come in for a cup of tea, dear?' I know I shook my head at that. And left without another word.

Hours later, after scraping together what money I could find, I arrived at the airport with a passport and an open mind. I landed in Lanzarote. It was a world away from our grey little island. And you. Neither of us thought I'd have the guts, but I guess it's easier when you're pretending to be someone else. Stepping off the plane into such sunlight and humidity was like crawling from a cave. At first, I wanted to retreat. But then I began to explore freedom. I listened to waves lapping while browning on the beach. I read. Ate. Slept.

'How brave,' said the party animals in the neighbouring apartment, when they realized I was holidaying alone.

I drank and danced with them. Sat at a bar, I swear a cute boy smiled at me.

'Want a drink?' he yelled over the synthesisers. I shook my head, my limit already exceeded. He leant over, musky aftershave, his lips by my ear. 'How about a dance?'

It was too hot. Uncomfortably close. The air thick. It had to break. I thought of you.

CONTROL

'Gotta go.'

I left him shrugging his shoulders and stumbled back, the soles of my high heels sticking to my feet. I hid in my bedroom as lightning flashbulbed the sky and thunder boomed. Like a developing photograph, you emerged slowly from the shadows. My tears flowed as freely as the rain.

'Why can't you leave me alone?'

I clenched a fist so hard that my false nails drew blood. Threw a glass against a wall. Pounded the bed. I wanted the world to break with me.

'Why me?'

I couldn't sleep with you there. My gloom in the next day's sunshine was as out of place as a pallbearer at a wedding. I cut the break short. You accompanied me on the flight home. How naïve was I to think you'd just leave me alone? You're never free from such tyranny. You seduced your way back into my consciousness. And like an addict, the temptation to surrender to something so intoxicating is always there. I suppose, despite everything, I couldn't be without you. We'd been together for so long that you were all I knew. Comfort in familiarity. Fear of the unknown. You took over. My worst enemy my only friend, working insidiously from the inside.

'You're weak, stupid and worthless,' you told me. Any mantra repeated enough will be believed.

I reached my 30s, shipwrecked from society. You can't drift anymore, when you've run aground. Entombed inside my bedsit, benefits swallowed by rent and bills and any savings long wasted, happiness was as far away as the holiday island.

'You'll never be rid of me,' rang through my head.

I had only one option left. I piled the pills on my bed. Just swallow and it's over. Couldn't do it.

I trudged to a motorway bridge. Headlights sparkled below. I longed to be swept away in their flow. As I looked down I saw Mother standing over my broken body. She was actually crying. I stepped away. At the bottom of the darkest pit was a kernel of light. I called her. Then hung up before she answered. Mother barged her way into my home, trying to mask her disgust at the clutter and dirt: all those unwashed pots and plates, unopened post and piles of clothes.

'Oh, Sarah.' I wasn't used to her eyes locking on mine. To the concern swimming inside them.

'Nothing's wrong,' I said. But everything was.

She grabbed my arms. Held me up as if I were wilting. 'You need help.'

I was too tired to resist. It was time for a divorce.

She separated us like a boxing referee. Moved me back in with her. Fed me nutritious food. Made sure I drank two litres of water a day. Became a scarecrow watching over me. Insisted I exercised. Took me to a doctor. Ensured I took each pill. Paid for a counsellor. And joined in with the mindfulness sessions. That kernel grew. She helped untangle it from your ensnaring roots. Made me realise that if I couldn't chop you down, then I'd rise above you to reach the sunshine that you blocked. As my confidence blossomed, I rejoined the human race, running hard to catch up. I returned to my friends and felt able to talk about you, rather than deny. Sat in a café with Andrew, he told me about the pain of being made redundant and the relief of finding another job. It was then that I realised I'd inherited my father's absence and my mother's disregard.

'I'm so sorry,' I said, crestfallen. 'That I wasn't there for you.'

He smiled. 'Don't worry.' And took my hand. 'It's just good to have you back.' He held it for a little longer than necessary, his skin warm on mine. It felt good.

When Mother deemed me better, she let me return home, though visited me regularly. In her autumnal garden we surveyed her sunflowers, the tallest a good foot below her previous best. The large browning heads nodded downwards, mildew mottling withered leaves.

'I'll have to remove them,' she said. 'The seeds and stems emit a toxin that inhibits the growth of other plants.' She looked mournful. I stroked her back, like a groom to an agitated horse.

Her ashen face brightened. 'I'll try again next year.' She turned to me. 'Maybe it's something we can do together?' I beamed, then faltered. Felt you lurking in the shade, knowing you'll always be there, waiting patiently, ready to emerge when you sense I'm weakening.

Mother pushed a piece of torn newspaper into my hand. 'An ad. For a job. Trainee hairdresser. You could give it a go.' I looked at the sunflowers. At how tall and strong she'd helped them grow. 'I'd like that.'

I felt lighter. I appreciated then, how I'd learnt how to live with you at my shoulder. And that's enough. Sometimes you're closer, but I'm ready. I know what you're capable of; I survived your worst. And I know you'll never go completely, but I also recognise how far I've come.

You have no form, no substance. You're nothing but a ghost. You may haunt me all my life. But I have you under control.

Sweetpea

by Eimear Arthur

They would not grow. She had kept the soil moist since sowing the seedlings, and she'd taken measures to protect against slugs and birds; but still, the sweet pea would not grow. Cara felt they were punishing her, taking vengeance against her for knocking against the table she was working on when repotting them; scattering earth and their tiny bodies across her balcony's floor. Maybe she had killed them all?

She Googled. Apparently, her plants could be suffering from "transplant shock": a potentially fatal state of arrested development. Following the directions online, she dutifully mixed a weak sugar solution and poured it over the pots, wondering if the soil could now be considered 'sodden'; another potential form of horticide.

Each footstep was a hollow slap as she descended the stairs of her building, rubbish bag in hand. All of the surfaces were reflective and hard – selected for an appearance of quality – but at less than five years old, they had begun to peel and crack. Cara remembered the threshold stone to her college in Oxford, its pale golden smoothness earned over hundreds of years. Tossing the bag in the bin outside, she noticed the sun on her skin; it was warm. She checked her app. Fifteen degrees Celsius. It had been 15 degrees below freezing last week. Spring at home was a gradual lightening of days, a lengthening of evenings, an incremental build to summer's crescendo.

Here in New York, spring was more of a concept than an experience; a moment you could easily miss if you weren't paying attention. She tried to be grateful that the cold had passed – the days when her ears and her fingers and even her nostrils went painfully numb – but she dreaded the slick, sticky days to come; the airless subway platforms and the carriage poles wet with other people's sweat. Which of the settlers had decided this was a habitable landscape, anyway? Too hot in summer, too cold in winter, mosquitos bloody everywhere. The settlers should have kept going. Why couldn't New York be in Washington? Maybe she should move to Washington.

Last spring, she had welcomed the incoming summer with delight, like a cat turning its head to the sun. It was all new and exciting then, the land of hope and opportunity. The world was hers. She hadn't yet experienced the air thickening with the smell of garbage on a summer's afternoon; the heavy, odorous cloak of humidity draping itself over everything.

She had not yet been forced to slow down in order to let a large Lower East Side rat cross her path, like it was exercising an established right of way. She had not yet appreciated that, in a place where strangers' arms touched her arms every day on public transport – sometimes unnecessarily, causing her to "accidentally" jab them with an elbow – she might long to feel skin on hers. But that was last spring; nothing had happened yet.

She arrived about five minutes late to meet Sarah at the place with the shuffleboard and the dogs in the backyard. Sarah stirred her Bloody Mary with its paper straw but didn't take a sip. Cara had long suspected that Sarah didn't like Bloody Marys at all, but that she was intent on cultivating the persona of someone who would like a Bloody Mary. Sarah stood to greet her, kissing Cara on the cheek one, two, three times.

'Three? Was that the number now?' Cara wondered, as they sat down. Sarah stirred her drink again – no sip this time either – and began a story, as she tore her napkin into tiny squares. The squares were relatively consistent in size and proportion; only a few having been misshapen through misjudgement of force or direction. The accreting pile of napkin-squares was comforting, and Cara watched it for a

minute or two before realising that she'd missed most of
what Sarah was saying. It sounded as if Kevin had ended
things, again, and it seemed that he had been particularly
cruel in doing so this time.

Cara felt a strange mix of sympathy – being dumped is
not fun for anyone – and revulsion. Some people present
a composed, even happy face to the world, while silently
crumbling inside. Others let it all ooze out of them, like pus
from an infected wound. Sarah was oozing. Cara scratched
the neck of the dachshund next to her, seeking distraction.
It writhed appreciatively but did not turn its head; it was
engrossed in something it held between its front paws. A
toy, perhaps, or maybe a bone. Nodding in the appropriate
places while Sarah spoke, Cara fixated on the dog and
its fixation, directing her finger strokes so it might turn
its head. Without warning, the dog succumbed to a fit of
sneezing and stood up to shake it off. Where its paws had
been was the tiny, blood-streaked carcass of a nestling; a
puny breastbone poking through its flesh.

Her vision blurred slightly as she stared, her lips began
to tingle and burn. She jerked her head to glare expectantly
at the murderous dachshund's owner, but he was too
engrossed in flirtation with a petite brunette to meet her
gaze. Her flush rising; Cara caught Sarah's eye and looked
pointedly at the chick's corpse, inviting her friend to share
in her outrage. 'Ugh, gross', Sarah offered, and finally took
a sip of her drink. A drop of the red liquid lingered on her
lip for second, before she launched into a detailed analysis
of which of Kevin's female friends he was probably sleeping
with.

Paul never cheated on Cara, she knew that. She wasn't
sure how or why she could be certain of his fidelity, but she
was. It wasn't so much that she thought he was some great
honourable being beyond temptation or impulse, or that
she thought their love was some special bubble, impervious
to damage. She just couldn't imagine him possessing the
industriousness to follow through on a flirtation.

Paul was the type of person to be content with 'good enough' – and what they'd had was certainly 'good enough'. He wouldn't have bothered risking it in pursuit of something better or more exciting. There was a safety in his laziness; his contentedness. She'd been happy in it, with him. Sarah had started to sob, taking giant, greedy gulps of air as she read aloud her last text conversation with Kevin. Cara saw the disinterested dog owner and his flirty friend exchange a glance.

She suddenly felt protective of her friend, and guilty for not paying the conversation more attention. It was becoming more and more difficult to exist outside of her own head these days. Everything seemed to reside on the other side of a smudged screen; one cloudy with fingerprints and grease marks. She reached across and squeezed Sarah's hand.

'Come on, let's go to mine. I have wine. You hungry?' she asked, soothingly. Sarah shrugged, then gave a little nod, trying to compose herself while patting the dampness under her eyes carefully with her ring fingers.

'Great. I have stuff for a stir-fry. Let's go', Cara said, shooting a last disparaging look at the dog and its owner as she stood up. The dachshund was sniffing its master's feet; the dead nestling was nowhere to be seen. Cara shuddered, then shook it off, turning to smile brightly at her friend.

'Let's go,' Sarah said.

***

Cara woke the next morning to a familiar sensation: that her brain was trying to dislodge itself from its position inside her skull. She cupped her head in her hands, then luxuriated in a yawn, stretching her limbs out to their extremities. Exhaling, she rolled over, and noted – not for the first time – the emptiness of her bed. She had grown used to sharing, to leaving space for somebody else. When would her sleeping body catch up, she wondered? She rolled into the middle of the bed and spread herself out like a starfish. For a while, she lay there, her eyes following a spider working furiously on a web that hung from her lampshade. It was focused, sure of its purpose.

Remembering Sarah – her guest – Cara pulled her unwilling body from where it lay and stood up. The veneered flooring felt cold and dusty underfoot. She remembered that she needed to sweep, or vacuum, or hire a cleaner. She had remembered that yesterday, as well. She picked a pair of sweatpants from the pile on the chair and pulled them on, then reached to open her window. Her bedroom smelled like sweat and stale regret. Vacuuming might help that, too. Tomorrow.

'Sarah?' she called out, pulling a t-shirt over her head as she walked. 'Sarah, you want a coffee?'

Sarah wasn't where Cara had left her, on the couch, under the cashmere blanket Paul's mother had given them as a housewarming gift. The blanket was now resting on the arm of the couch, neatly folded. Cara flicked the switch on the coffee pot and went back to the bedroom to check her phone. A text from Sarah:

'Sorry, couldn't sleep so headed home. Thanks for last night: needed to vent. Let's hang soon! Xx' Cara welcomed the reprieve from having to play hostess for the morning, and switched on the TV while she stacked dishes next to the sink. She needed to leave soon, anyway.

**

Cara waited at the doorway, wondering if she should ring the bell again or not. Had she heard it buzz the first time? She hadn't been paying attention. Two little boys tore past, shrieking and laughing.

'Wellington!' a curly-haired woman with a Trader Joe's shopping bag called after them 'Welly, stop teasing your brother'. An attractive older man who looked a little like the guy from Jurassic Park – what was his name, not

Jeff Goldblum...Sam Neill! – sat on the next stoop over, smoking a cigarette. Cara breathed the second-hand smoke in deeply, gratefully. She should never have given up.

His eyes met hers and they exchanged the sort of gentle, apologetic smiles strangers give each other when they both try to use a doorway at the same time, or step into the same line in the supermarket. Cara looked at the bell again. Should she ring –

'Cara, hello, great to see you! Is that a plant?' Jane's husband, Dave, had answered the door. Dave, though he almost exclusively spoke politely – even warmly – to her, had a knack of conveying complete disinterest in and detachment from Cara and anything she had to say. She was not sure if this was intentional or not. He had, however, noticed the plant. She had thought this was a better present for a pregnant person than wine.

'Come on, we are all in the back,' Dave said, leading her through a hallway filled with family photos and wedding-gift paintings and a full storage wall. The storage wall was built-in – custom, probably, Cara thought – and was painted one of those deep jewel-toned green-blues that only expensive paint brands make well. 'Jane, it's Cara,' Dave announced. 'She brought a plant.'

'Cara, drink?' He asked.

'I'll grab some water, please' she said, 'I can get it myself?'

'Ok, great. Work away.' Dave walked to the fridge to retrieve a couple of beers, setting the offending plant on the island as he passed it. Then, he walked out through the French doors into the garden, where Cara could see a couple of male figures through the glass.

'Cara!' There was genuine warmth in Jane's voice, there always was. Jane was sitting with a group of five or six women Cara recognized from the wedding, or from social media. Lucy had been with them on that couples' weekend upstate. A toddler was walking from one end of the room to the other, holding an adult with one hand and a red wooden block with the other. Two smaller children sat on a rubber mat next to the women, surrounded by brightly-coloured books and balls. Jane, with one hand on her belly and the other on the chair, slowly eased herself up from where she sat, a broad smile on her face. Cara walked to her, arms outstretched, and the friends hugged. Jane smelled of vanilla and washing detergent.

'You look amazing', Cara said, because it was true - but also because she knew it was something she was expected to say.

'Amazing!' Lucy agreed, standing to kiss Cara on the cheek. 'How are you, honey?' Cara smiled at Lucy, who looked older than she remembered, but not worse for it.

'I was so sorry to hear about you and Paul,' A sympathetic smile, to accompany words that felt like a slap.

'Yes, well, these things happen,' Cara spoke breezily, quickly, as if recalling a dry-cleaning mishap. 'And how have you been?'

Lucy gave a knowing chuckle. 'Well! It has been the most challenging year of my life, of course. But also, the most rewarding.' Cara felt momentarily confused; was there was something she was missing? Then she followed Lucy's eyeline, to where Caroline – or Carol? – sat with a tiny figure in blue lying prone on her chest. Carol/ine mouthed a greeting, which Cara returned.

'Of course! The baby! Congratulations!'

'Adam,' Lucy smiled.

'Tiny Adam.' Cara felt a swelling sensation in her stomach, which rose to her chest. Her throat tightened a little. 'He's...'

'He's six weeks,' Lucy offered, 'A hungry little man! Relentless. But it's so worth it, of course.'

'Of course!' Cara imagined the relentlessness of it; the waking every few hours during the night, the swollen breasts and cracked nipples and rising panic at their cries of pain from trapped wind. Then, the smell of a newborn's head, the comfort of their weight in your arms, the closeness of their soft skin on yours.

'I keep telling Jane to bank whatever sleep she can now! I used to think I knew what tired was. I had no idea!'

Cara felt tired and hot, as if last night's Pinot Grigio was liberating itself via her pores. She accepted a seat when one was offered to her and concentrated on sipping water and keeping her conversation light. She tried to imagine feeling more tired than she did now, and she remembered a day in the hospital in December when she had bled and bled.

Two of the women were discussing their predictions for the New York housing market and what areas would gentrify next. Cara felt her attention drifting, but she smiled and made affirmative noises in what she hoped were the right places.

'Would you like to hold him?' Carol/ine was bobbing above her.

Cara would like that. She stood up, nodding enthusiastically. Maybe too enthusiastically, she thought, and caught herself. 'That would be nice.' She held out her arms to receive his tiny body.

'Maybe you should sit down? It's…it can be easier' Lucy said, with a tight smile. Cara resisted rolling her eyes, and sat, obediently, as the baby was bequeathed to her. Lucy was watching, hovering: 'Just make sure to support his head,' she half-whispered, her sentence trailing into nothing once she saw that Cara's hold was appropriately supportive. Adam smelled warm and milky and pure. Cara watched his chest rise and fall and tried to match the rhythm of her breathing to his. The pace of inhalation was quicker than felt natural, but still it calmed her.

Lucy joined the gentrification conversation, but still she kept an eye on Cara. Cara resented the intrusion, the undercurrent of mistrust. And yet, she didn't fully trust herself. She imagined a moment's distraction; little Adam falling from her arms to the terrazzo floor. The impact would surely shatter… definitely damage. She shook the image from her head. A tiny carcass. There would be hysteria and rage and they would blame her. Why would she even think the thought?

She had read somewhere – or maybe heard, on a podcast – that these kinds of thoughts; these terrifying impulses like the urge to jump in front of an incoming L train, were, in fact, the mind's way of protecting you from danger. That wanting to jump really meant you wanted to live, or something. She wouldn't let any harm come to little Adam; she would protect him.

'You're a natural,' Jane whispered, and Cara loved her for it, despite fearing her friend was wrong. Maybe she wasn't a natural? Maybe that was what the whole thing had been about? She knew this was irrational – she was being irrational, Paul had said that, trying to comfort her – but how did anyone know it wasn't something she had done? How could anyone really know?

She had been so wound up, excited about their little secret – it had been a secret; it was too soon to tell people maybe that had had something to do with it? Lucy was watching her again. Cara looked down at Adam quickly, and up Lucy again, smiling her congratulations. Was Lucy's body a more hospitable environment than hers?

Cara breathed in the smell of him, took stock of his tiny soft squares of fingernails, the downy softness of the hair on his head. He felt much heavier now; his weight and that of her own body suddenly barely bearable. She smiled again at Lucy at returned the child to his mother's arms.

'He's beautiful,' she said. 'Congratulations.'

That night, at home, Cara mixed a weak sugar solution and poured it over her pots. She sat on her balcony and hoped that they would grow.

A Bowl of Pho

by Belinda Weir

I had no idea when I met Linh that she would spend the
rest of her life with me.She was very beautiful.

'Out of your league, Bao,' I thought to myself. I had no
hope of attracting her, so I was able to be myself with Linh.
I made her laugh. Silly jokes – taking a coin out of my bag
and making it disappear, only to "find" it again nestling in
her trouser pocket. Making fart noises so everyone thought
the guy next to me had broken wind, that sort of thing. It
was worth the possibility of getting into trouble, just to hear
Linh giggle. They say that women like men who are funny,
provided they are not fat as a porker and ugly as Uncle
Wen I suppose. What do I know? I have not known many
women, but even I could tell that Linh was special.

I saw her properly just twice, once when we boarded
and again when we stopped, and it was dark both times,
with only brief shafts of sudden moonlight, but her face is
burned in my memory. Her hair hung straight and fine in
a bob that stopped just short of her jawline, and her fringe
was long so that she seemed to peep from under it, with
big eyes, black and shiny as molasses. Her skin was smooth
and pale as buttermilk. I thought when I first saw her that
she was a little chubby. It was surprising – her bulky arms
and tummy seemed at odds with the bird-like wrists and
slender fingers that emerged from the cuffs of her pink
jumper.

'I put on all my clothes,' she confided. 'I didn't want to
leave any behind, and I thought it might be cold in London.'

That explained why she felt so soft when I put my arm
around her. She was padded like a marshmallow – a vest,
a long-sleeved blue t-shirt, then a green silk blouse with
a peter pan collar, a white collarless shirt over that, then

the pink jumper and finally a huge waterproof jacket like a quilt, black so that it didn't reflect light, and with a hood to cover her face. In the darkness I could feel her breath on my cheek when she turned to whisper to me, and when she lay her head down on my shoulder to sleep, I could sense her heart beating, just a few centimetres away from mine.

'Where are you from?' she asked me. She spoke in a low voice but even so, someone at the other side admonished her. 'Quiet!'

The unit was sealed; nothing could get in or out and unless we stood up and started banging on the walls, nobody would know we were in there. We had been told to make no sound, no noise at all. I knew that if anyone heard us, they might send us home and all the waiting and the planning, the hard work and the saving, the goodbyes and good luck conversations, all of it would have been for nothing. But it made no difference because Linh couldn't stop talking. Every few seconds a thought would occur to her, which she had to share.

'Do you think we'll see the Queen when we get to London?' she asked me.

Then, a little later, 'I will get a job in a bar when we get there. There are lots of bars, and they pay well, Tranh said.'

Tranh was her brother. Linh had told me, in an earlier burst of confidence, that he did not have a proper job, but worked at the beach bar, collecting glasses, washing up, stacking away the wooden tables and chairs. It was his idea, Linh told me, that she should make the journey first. They had saved tips for a long time, Linh said. She had told me many things about herself during the long journey, while I had shared nothing. My brother impressed that on me when I called to say goodbye. He silently ladled me a bowl straight from the huge restaurant wok. I wanted to enjoy the pho, savour the juicy chicken, the crunch of the sprouts, the sharp eye-watering bite of the spring onion. But there was no time. I shovelled the chewy noodles into my mouth, trying not to slurp the salty broth, and even so I splashed a little on my t-shirt.

'Keep your head down Bao, okay? Just keep your mouth shut and you'll be fine,' Huy instructed.

Head down, mouth shut. Right. After a pause, when I was turning my attention once more to chasing the last bite of chicken round the bowl, he said,

'You're on your own, Bao. Don't forget that. Don't trust anyone. 'He punched me on my shoulder, and said, 'Take it easy, man,' and went back to his cooking. I smiled in the darkness – I could almost taste that pho.

Linh turned around, shifting her weight to lean in closer to me, so we were curled up like spoons. It was not because she liked me, she said, but because she was cold. We all were, at first, freezing, and Linh, beneath all her tops and shirts, was thin too. Tiny.

'If you won't tell me anything about you, tell me a story. I'm scared,' she said.

'No Linh. We really shouldn't be talking,' I scolded her.

Linh sniffed and said, into the darkness, 'I thought we were going to be friends. I will tell you about my life then, Mr Boring. And no, you will not shhh me. I like to talk – it stops my teeth from chattering. I come from a little fishing village in the north. It is – it used to be – very beautiful, a lovely place. We have long beaches of fine soft sand, like palm sugar, the greenest sea and the nicest people. Everyone knows everyone. Everyone talks to anyone, there are no strangers in my village. Even in the summer, when there are tourists, it's a good place to live.

My father is a fisherman – or he was for a long time, and my brother, Tranh, was too. Every morning they would sail out, very early, when the sky was still dark and only the tiniest hint of morning on the horizon, in daddy's little wooden boat, to catch fish. I would go down to the shore to watch them casting off sometimes.'

The guy on my other side was listening too. I could hear his breathing slowing down – he had been very scared when we first climbed in, almost crying, and I think he would have run off if the driver hadn't picked him up by the collar and pretty much thrown him into the van like a sack of beets.

'Too late for second thoughts,' the driver had said. Now the boy lay curled up on his side, and he shuffled across the floor till his back was against my leg for warmth. I pushed him away a little – I only wanted to feel Linh close to me. It was not polite of me, I know that, and I wish I had been kinder.

'There isn't much to do in the village, but that's okay,' said Linh. 'Mum died when I was quite little, so I look after the house, I do the cooking and take Minh to school, I clean a bit, work in a bar sometimes in the evening, watch TV – the usual kind of thing.'

'Is that why you left? It was dull?'

I was interested, despite myself.

I felt Linh stiffen next to me. 'It wasn't dull,' she corrected me. 'Peaceful. Nice. I liked it.' She was quiet for a few minutes.

'So...'

'So, there was an accident a few months ago – a chemical spill from one of the factories somewhere further up the coast. We didn't find out for a while, but the fish started dying. They floated in on every tide, thousands of them, bellies up and gasping. Papa said we couldn't eat them. He couldn't catch healthy fish so that was that. No more work for Daddy or for Tranh. And no tourists because the beaches were spoiled. So, no money.'

Linh said nothing again for a long while. She pulled her knees up to her chin and rested her head on them. I thought maybe she was crying but if she was, she at least did it silently. After a few minutes she turned her head, and I could feel her looking at me.

'Still, new life, eh?' I could tell she was smiling.

'Yes,' I said.

For what felt like hours then, there was silence. We lay still, waiting. Listening. I allowed myself to feel the warmth of Linh next to me, imagined that it could go on, that we would be friends after our journey ended. She will need a friend, I thought, and why not Bao? She had grown to trust me in the tiny space of time we had been together, and I thought we could spent the rest of our lives together. If not as a boyfriend, I could be like a brother to her. I did not want to be on my own, that's the truth. I must have slept eventually because I dreamed about my mother. She was cooking in the tiny kitchen, using the only ring that worked; the burners were clogged, and the flames sputtered and danced under the wok. She turned to me, smiled, and pulled me to her for a hug.

'My Bao,' she whispered. She hugged me closer, and then tighter, crushing me, making it difficult to breathe. When I fought my way out of sleep and opened my eyes to the blackness, I realized that part of the dream was true – I was finding it hard to catch a breath. I stood up, my head swimming, tried to bang on the side of the van.

There was a rasping noise behind me, one of the others whispering,

'I can't breathe. Help.'

I wanted to help. But I had no strength for anything; as weak as a drowning kitten, I had just enough time to lower myself to the floor, wrap my arms around Linh and hope that dying wouldn't hurt too much, before everything went black. I really don't remember anything after that. Not until I woke up in the hospital. It seems I was one of the fortunate ones, although I don't feel lucky. They are planning to send me back, as soon as I am well enough to travel. Sooner, probably. I overheard the nurses talking next to my bed last night.

'Imagine, dying like that. Far away from home, in the dark, among strangers. Whatever would make you do such a thing?' I wanted to say something, but I didn't want them to know I could understand what they were saying.

'The girl he was with,' said the nurse, not looking at me as she attached a bag of fluid to the pole at the head of the bed. 'Do you think she was his girlfriend?'

And that is how I learned that Linh was dead. The women looked at each other; the younger one shook her head. They both finished what they were doing without speaking and went away to attend to other patients.

Later in the evening the older nurse came back, holding a plastic bag. She pulled the curtains shut around my bed and handed it to me silently; I expected food, maybe a book or some soap perhaps. It wasn't soap. Or food. Inside the bag were Linh's clothes: a vest, a long-sleeved blue t-shirt, a green silk blouse with a peter pan collar, a white collarless shirt, a pink jumper and, on the top, a waterproof jacket, size large, black and padded. The nurse left, and I got up. I took the drip from my arm and I found my jeans and t-shirt in the grey metal locker next to the bed.

I put those on, catching the faintest scent of sour, salty noodle broth as I pulled the t-shirt over my head. Over the top I slipped on Linh's jacket. I gathered the hood around my face and waited until I could hear that the nurses were busy with the old man who was dying, quietly, in the room next door. I picked up the bag, walked down the rubber floor of the corridor in bare feet, pressed the button to release the door, and stepped out into the night.

One day I will go to Linh's village, and I will tell her father, and Tranh, that Linh told me all about them and how much she loved them, and that when Linh died, she was excited and happy and looking forward to a new life. And she was among friends. Till then, I will wear her jacket. I don't think she would mind.

Scattered from the Mountain

by Thandi Sebe

It was almost 35 years to the day that his father had told
him that he wanted to be cremated. At the time, H had just
started discovering the wonders of masturbation, and so
death was the furthest thing from his mind when his father
brought up the topic at breakfast between coffee and toast.
It took H a moment to understand what his father was
talking about, steering – with great effort – his thoughts
away from the magazine cover he had caught a glimpse
of in a shop window, making sure to save the image in his
mind for later use. Instead of answering his father's request
with a 'Yes, daddy' as a good, obedient son would have
done, he responded like this:

'Why?'

To which his father replied:

'I want you to scatter my ashes from the top of Table
Mountain.'

'Why?'

'Because I've never been up.'

'Why don't you go up now?'

'Because,' his father took a brief but noticeable pause
here to indicate that he was about to say something that his
son would not like, 'I have to work hard to put food on the
table for your greedy stomach, and there is no time to go up
there.'

'Ugh,' he uttered - or perhaps a similar teenage sound -
but he knew that it was true.

His father continued talking, but H failed miserably at
pushing aside the re-emerging images, and so his father's
voice drifted somewhere into the ethers of his mind,

almost inaudible, until decades later when his father's wish suddenly became important to remember. For a teenager raised in the 80s, H and his father had a rather open relationship, one where 'talking back', so long as it contained humour or wit, was not punished by lashings, like in some of the other households H had witnessed. In fact, H knew a number of families in his neighbourhood where 'being clever' seemed a sin and was punished quite unimaginatively by a clap with a shoe or a lashing with a branch, or if those were not within reach, with the slap of a bare hand. H had only ever been hit once. He had used a then rather often used word denoting a specific group of people, and he had done so without any malicious intent, but merely to set apart one person from another, in a rather banal situation he was trying to describe. But his cheek stung badly as he looked in shock at his father who seemed equally surprised, as though he was not responsible for the red demarcation of a hand now clearly contouring H's face. After the first moment of shock had worn off, his father whispered into the awkward silence,

'Don't ever try to put yourself above someone else.' And that was all he said before disappearing out of the front door. He did not speak to his son until the following day, when he enquired about who had eaten the last koesister he had so looked forward to. They never spoke about the incident.

Only now, 35 years later, with his father on his death bed – a couch placed in the centre of the living room, from which he had a perfect view of the living room, the kitchen and the flowering hibiscus tree through the window facing the yard – did H suddenly understand the significance of that face slap. He was busy frying some eggs when his mind revisited the old memory, and suddenly understood the meaning of what had occurred that day. His father had not hurried out of the house because he had been annoyed or angry, but because he had felt two separate instances of shame. One, for having failed to raise a son who was aware of his place in the world and could utter such a painful word so easily; and two, because he had failed for the first time in his life to restrain his own anger.

When H's mind returned to the present moment and to his eggs, he saw that they had burned to a blistering crust. He threw them into the yard for the dogs to eat and decided to apologise to his father for having ever housed that word in his mouth. His father appreciated the gesture and in turn apologised for having raised his hand at him that day. All things now settled, and no regrets or secrets left to share, H thought that perhaps this meant his father could leave his physical restraints, plagued by pains, behind and move on peacefully to the next level. But he lived for another 58 days after that and, having nothing more revelatory to say, the following weeks were spent mainly telling jokes or reminiscing about the nice things that existed in the bad old days. Like summer holidays enjoyed at over-crowded beaches, trying to stand knee deep in the shallow end of the ocean without getting brain freeze.

Then, suddenly, 58 days later, when H had become so used to his father being on his death bed that it no longer seemed like a death bed at all, he was gone. H had just gotten up from the sofa and walked to the kitchen to fetch his father some more sugar for his cup of Rooibos tea ('One more spoon of sugar won't kill me!') when he remembered a joke he had read in the newspaper that day, that he thought his father might appreciate. He traced his steps back to the living room to present the joke, only to find his father gone. Not that his body had physically disappeared, but H sensed instantly that his father's body was ... well, empty. He wouldn't have been able to describe it other than in that way; that he looked distinctly 'without a soul'. Gone. Just like that.

H had thought somehow that it would be more dramatic, the ending. He had not expected a fade out like in one of those mediocre plays or films where the final scene comes on suddenly and leaves one sitting incredulously, waiting for something more to happen, until the credits roll in and force you to accept that it is over. H had expected more of the ending. And just like a theatre audience that slowly and awkwardly realises that it is now expected to clap, the realisation dawned on H that he too was expected to do something. But he wasn't sure what that was. Surely not clap. Call the doctors? The ambulance? Or sit down next to his father and maybe gently hold his hand in case some part of him was still present and needed comfort during his transition?

He decided to do the latter, and so he sat down beside him on the floor and slid his own hand into his father's, dangling off the couch by his side. H had never realised how large his father's hands were. Much larger than his own. It made him feel like a child, which was most likely also the only other time they had ever held hands like this. Unsure of what to do, he told his father the joke anyway. He realised as he told it that it was not really that funny after all, and so he was hardly surprised after delivering the punchline, that there was no reaction.

After a few moments of silence, he placed a kiss gently on his father's head, and then felt with surprise that a tear rolled down his cheek, although he had promised his father not to cry. Not because his father was of the old-school conviction that a man should never make use of his tear ducts, that they served a purely decorative function, but because he believed that there is nothing worth crying about when a man who has lived a good life dies at such an old age.

H made to wipe the tear away quickly, but he was too slow, and it landed on his father's cheek. This made H cry even more because now it looked like his father was crying, and that was a painful sight. When H was finished, he discovered he wasn't sure how long he should sit like this to honour the occasion. The question was answered by a pain in his knee, and he got up slowly, realising that he was also no longer young, and he imagined himself lying there in his father's place, with his own two daughters watching his empty body. He shook his head, called his father's doctor, and then his mother, and then that was that.

And now he was here, walking up bloody Table Mountain in the midday heat, cursing his father for having died in the middle of the hottest summer of the last decade. He wondered whether his father could have imagined that he would live 35 more years after declaring his cremation request, and whether he knew that it would mean H being an old man himself, struggling up a rocky path with two daughters in their pre-teen years, who verbalised their discomfort with every step. Right now, his daughters, not even halfway up the mountain, were hosting a minor strike.

'Daddy, it's too hot, I can't anymore. Can't we scatter them from here?' said T, who was by far the naughtier one. And he was tempted to do just that, but he made to honour his father's request and pushed them on.

'We're almost there, come, you're still young.' Again, T: 'If we make it to the top, you can cremate me too because I will be dead.' And she emphasised 'dead' in that teenager-esque tone; piercing yet bored. H had continued the tradition of his father, that children could 'talk back' so long that it was funny. Although what was considered funny, he acknowledged, differed sometimes according to age group.

'Move!' He pushed her lightly from the back, and she let him push her like that for a minute as they clambered up, out of breath and wondering how it could be that the higher they climbed, the further away the peak appeared. They took another break, although this one was unanimously decided upon.

'Water break!' shouted M, the younger daughter, his baby, and T immediately shifted swiftly towards the only speck of cool stone, shaded by a small shrub.

H didn't sit down, too worried that his knee would not allow for him to raise himself again without his daughters' help, and he knew they would not let an opportunity like that pass without cackling like evil twins about his old and broken body. A young attractive couple, moving with an ease that slightly enraged H, passed them by at that moment, and the woman smiled at his children laying there on the side of the narrow pathway.

'You look like you're having a great' time, she said knowingly to the two tired faces, as she tried not to step onto the backpack that T had dropped in the middle of the path.

'We're going up to scatter my grandpa's ashes. When my daddy was a boy, my grandpa said he wants them scattered from the top and he's not allowed to use the cable car, because he mustn't be lazy,' M had both a skill and a bad habit of opening up to strangers indiscriminatory.

'But my daddy is old and wants us to take breaks every two seconds,' T added to round off the story. At this point H dropped in a word.

'Stop embarrassing me in front of strangers.' The girls giggled at his feigned outrage, and it gave them the energy to continue their arduous hike up, only taking a break a few more times. These were mostly initiated by H pretending to call attention to the sound of a bird, or to take a moment to appreciate a particularly beautiful view. They played along, too exhausted now to make fun of his age, and perhaps becoming somewhat aware of the solemn silence that was spreading across the mountain as they reached the peak, a reminder of the task that lay before them. When they reached the top and saw the edge of the mountain and the city spread out below like a carpet, H wanted to high five his kids, but he didn't have the energy, and so he remained quiet. His daughters mistook this prolonged silence for solemnity and so they honoured what they believed to be a spiritual moment, and too did not speak. It was the wind that interrupted the stillness, a gush of cold air hitting them from behind suddenly and harshly, like an ungentle lover waking up a sleeping partner with an unfriendly nudge.

'Daddy, it's freezing,' the girls sang in unison, and H quickly, and without a word, pulled from his backpack the two jerseys that he had packed for his girls that morning. They had ignored his cautionary warning that it could get cold on the mountain, insisting instead that 'it's like a million degrees today!'. And of course, such is the life of a father, he had forgotten to pack something warm for himself while packing their bags. While his daughters put on their clothes (neglecting to thank him), H took the box out of the bag and was thankful that he had had the good foresight to pour the ashes from the urn to this light cardboard box. Gripping tightly to the box, he gently shoved the girls in the direction of where he believed his late father's house was. He cursed the wind, and simultaneously thanked it for propelling him slightly forward with its force. When M came to a halt and said, 'This is perfect!', he agreed.

It was perfect. There, below them to the left, lay Lion's Head, draped in fluffy clouds like candy floss, signifying a rainy day to follow this one. The rest of the city was cloudless. There, past Signal Hill, was Robben Island, like a single leaf lost in a large pond. The shoreline that stretched along, housing the wealthiest and the fittest people of this city. Further to the right was the view of the neighbourhood of his childhood.

From up there you could not tell how much it had changed, that the corner store where he used to stand and look at those magazine covers had shut down, making way for a lofty building that seemed to be an office space, café and apartment building at once. Or that the park, once home to a few local drug addicts, and a favoured hang-out spot for him and his friends, had been turned into another mall-like building with not one, but two coffee shops to satisfy the needs of the newly moved in caffeine-addicts. None of that was visible from up here. Just some tiny houses of white walls and red roofs that could be made out by his daughters, and speckles of blurry white and red made out by H, who desperately needed glasses.

'And now?' asked T. H carefully took the lid off the box.

He peaked inside. All that remained of his father was this dust, waiting to be returned to the universe.

'Now we scatter his ashes,' he said as he looked around to make sure that they were alone.

The cold had cleared the mountain and the few people in the distance were making their way to the Table Mountain shop, presumably to get some coffee. H took a deep breath, smiled at his daughters who had both begun to tear up, and then stretched out his hand holding the box and, slowly and deliberately, with as much devotion as possible, began to pour his father's remains into the wind to be carried into the distance. But H had miscalculated the wind's direction. He watched in horror as the ashes, instead of gracefully rolling down the edge of the mountain as he had envisaged, were propelled by a sudden gust of wind straight back into H and his daughters.

All three of them stood wide-eyed, frozen as the ashes whirled around their faces a couple of times. Then the gust was over, and the ashes settled, some on the ground before them, and some on H's collar and his daughters' hair. They stood silent like that a moment, shocked at how their little ceremony had been hijacked and ridiculed by the South Easterly wind.

Then T said, 'Oh my god!', dragging out the 'o' in 'God' very long, almost like she was pointing out who was responsible for this mess. It was then that H remembered how his father's speech had continued that day 35 years ago. His father had iterated that H should make sure to check the wind's direction before scattering his ashes into the wind. 'But of course, that goes without saying,' he had added.

Now H stood there with his father on his shoes, and he couldn't help but laugh, and once he started, he couldn't stop. His daughters joined in. Laughter turned to crying and back again, until the laughing and crying became indistinguishable. H hugged his daughters, who dug their heads into the comfort of his arms. They stood there for another couple of minutes like that in the cold, with H's arms wrapped around their shoulders, looking into the distance, each one thinking their own thoughts. Then they turned to make their way to the cableway in silence (permission had been granted to use the cable way on the way down!). H hastily paid for the tickets and they stood in line, which consisted of just the three of them.

'That was a bit more of a bang to the ending,' H thought to himself, and he wished his father could have been there to watch their spectacular mishap, knowing that it would have made him laugh. 'Hope you enjoyed the show,' he said quietly as they made their way back down into the city through the clouds.

PEACE UNTO THE HEATHEN

Peace Unto the Heathen

by Penny Frances

Your face lights up as we approach you, positioned ready in the armchair in your room.

'Ah!' you shake your head in wonder. Always the best bit of the visit; making it worthwhile, just in that moment.

'I don't think I knew you were coming,' you say as I lean to kiss you. Already that flicker of anxiety, not liking the not knowing.

'Look, I've brought Charlie.'

'Oh, Charlie! I didn't realize...' your sentence fades as your mind stretches to find what you didn't realize.

'Happy Christmas, Gran.' Charlie brushes his unshaven cheek against you.

'Is it Christmas?'

'Yes, you've got dressed up, see?' I admire the crushed velvet trouser suit: standard special occasion wear.

'I think I knew...' Your bright smile once more.

I pull off my coat, already suffocating in that sickly care home warmth.

'Look, we've brought crackers and presents, and some of Alex's Christmas cake.' I unpack my bag onto the bed.

Our festive efforts head immediately downhill with the crackers. Charlie tries to pull one with you, but you shake your head in an anxious spin, your breathing quickening.

'I, I don't. What-?'

'You have to pull it, here!' I put my hand over yours and give it a tug. The cracker comes apart, contents spilling onto your lap. You scowl up at me.

'It didn't bang!' I pull out the snap strip.

PEACE UNTO THE HEATHEN

'Mum, does it matter?' Charlie rolls his eyes.

I flash to when you still ruled Christmas in the early days after Daddy left. That year when our New Zealand cousin was there, along with Marion's husband for the first time. How you forced the jollity, insisting on games after dinner. Refusing to let our cousin drop out of Consequences: 'You must write something amusing!' It was years before either he or Marion's husband put in another Christmas appearance. And now here's me, shrieking at the lack of bangs, planting a paper hat on your head and making Charlie pull the other crackers with me. Am I trying to give you what I think you want? Or, worse, turning into you? Charlie reads a joke:

'What does Santa do with fat elves?'

'What did he say?' You frown and I repeat the joke louder.

'He sends them to an elf farm.' Charlie grins.

'Oh, that's pathetic,' your frown deepens. Total disapproval.

'It's a cracker joke!' I struggle to contain my exasperation.

Rosalie comes in with a tea tray and puts it on the occasional table with the ceramic top that Marion had renovated.

'Eliza, you are lucky, such a lovely family!' Rosalie beams. 'Your other daughter and her girls yesterday. Didn't I tell you today, Penelope's coming?' She gives you a friendly nudge.

'And where are you from?' Your best polite-to-stranger tone.

'The Philippines.' She runs her hand through grey-streaked bobbed hair, smooths her blue uniform over her wide hips.

'Yes, I think my sister, your family...we had a house, my father...' You pick at your scalp as you lose your thread.

'Look at you, all festive in your hats.' Rosalie steps back to admire us. 'Shall I take a photo?'

'Oh, yes,' I grab my phone. 'Come on Charlie, crouch down behind Gran,' I say, remembering how you used to boss us into formation for group photos.

'Where is Charlie?' you fret.

'Smile, Eliza!' calls Rosalie. I show you the photo, catch a whiff of BO. That trouser suit needs a visit to the cleaners.

'When was that?' You frown at the phone.

'Just now, see, there's Charlie.'

'Look at my terrible grey hair!'

True, you always coloured your hair. It's one of the things they have quietly let drop in the home, though you still have your wash and set every week. I can see the lotion applied to where you have picked away your hair follicles. Hair dye probably not the best idea.

Rosalie comes to look. 'Eliza, you look so young, doesn't she?'

'Yes, you still take a good photo.' I'll put it on Facebook, my friends will remark how happy we all look, it'll please my auntie in New Zealand.

'I don't like the yellow hat,' you say, shaking it at Rosalie as she backs out of the room. Yellow was your favourite colour: you could wear it, you would say, with your olive complexion.

'Would you prefer blue?' I offer my hat.

You snatch it from me, fiddle with the paper. I resist helping you, move the tea-things to the chest-of-drawers. I grimace at my reflection in your mirror: my skin flushed, the creases under my eyes just like yours. I pour the tea. Call Charlie over to take you a cup and some cake.

'Careful, you'll spill it!' you shout as he leans to put it on the table.

'It's fine, Gran. Here, let me do that.' Charlie takes the blue hat and places it on your head.

You keep rearranging your cup and plate while I settle in the other easy chair and Charlie on the antique dining chair Marion also got restored. Half your furniture was falling to bits by the time we moved you to the care home.

PEACE UNTO THE HEATHEN

But we pulled out the best small pieces and pictures, and to start with you would think you were in your house when we sat here with you. Now it seems your brain concocts a random version of where you are, based on whatever scraps of association happen to surface. A school staff room; a university halls of residence; a holiday hotel. Charlie and I have all but finished our tea and cake, while you still fuss with the plates.

'Come on, Mummy, you always like Alex's Christmas cake.' You break off a piece. 'What is this?' You frown at the glazed nut topping.

'It's an almond.'

'I don't think so. Is this tea?'

'Yes, have some tea,' I say, relieved when you actually take a gulp. 'Oh, I nearly forgot, your present.' I get up to fetch it from the bed.

'Is that for me?' Your eyes widen in what looks like mock surprise. Maybe it's just that you have pencil drawn above the line of your eyebrows.

You fiddle with the paper; admire the swirl of gold and blue holly. 'It's very smart wrapping!'

'Do you need a hand, Gran?' You give Charlie a puzzled frown but let him rip the paper. Eventually the present emerges.

'Hmm,' you turn it over and over.

'It's a CD, Handel's Messiah,' Charlie points to the cover.

'I noticed you haven't got a copy,' I say.

'Oh, no, I think my father... on the gramophone... last time...' Yes, it was our grandfather, East Ender made good, who gifted you your love of music. The radiogram in their living room, belting out Verdi and Puccini.

'Would you believe they didn't have it in HMV?' I say. 'I had to order it on the internet.'

You read the cover: '*Colin Davis; London Symphony Orchestra...Susan Gritton...*I don't think they're wellknown.'

'You know Colin Davis? I made sure I chose a decent

recording.' I rejected the cheaper versions thinking you would be snobby about them.

I put the first CD on the portable player. The slow weight of the overture filters through, the sound not as full as I'd hoped for. I turn it up slightly, sit back down as the pace quickens with the violin section.

'Can you hear it OK?' I ask as your face creases with frowning.

'What is this terrible noise?'

'It's the Messiah.'

Your mouth puckers. 'It's nothing like the one I know.'

I take a deep breath. 'It's just the overture, it'll get going in a minute.'

'Have I had any tea?' I give you a re-fill as the tenor solo starts with the sustained notes of Comfort ye My people.

'You know it now, *that her iniquity is pardoned...*' I sing with the repeated line.

'What is it? It sounds terrible,' you say.

'You'll recognise it when the chorus comes in.'

You start fiddling again with the almond on your cake. 'What is this peculiar thing?'

'It's a nut, leave it. Just eat the cake.'

'I don't think it's very nice.'

I pull back from repeating that you've always liked Alex's Christmas cake. Charlie shrugs with a resigned smile.

'Charlie's just finished his first term at university.' The well-tested tactic of using news of grandchildren as a diversion.

'Oh, I didn't know...'

'Tell Gran.'

'Er, yeah, I'm at Manchester Met doing history,' he mumbles.

'Where?' You look at me to interpret.

'You need to speak up, and slow down,' I tell Charlie.

'Manchester Met,' he tries again.

'Manchester Metropolitan, it's the old poly,' I explain.

'I don't think...what are you studying?'

'History.'

'Oh, terribly difficult. All those dates!'

Charlie smiles. 'I find it interesting.'

'I always loved history, just an everlasting story,' I add.

'My history teacher tried to persuade me to take it for School Cert; they all wanted me, because I was intelligent, you see?' You treat Charlie to a superior look and his lips twitch with holding in his grin. 'But I said, no, all those dates!'

One of the well-rehearsed stories of your brilliant youth. Best marks in Essex for School Cert. Marion and I joke that you peaked at 16, never got over it. But now this is unusually coherent, compared to the muddle your past has become, with me present during the war, my house apparently familiar from your childhood. We drift into silence as the music launches into a new chorus.

'Here you go, Mummy, you'll remember this bit.' I sing along, *'for unto us a Child is bororrororororororn...'*

You tense up your shoulders. 'What is this terrible noise?'

'The Messiah, you know?'

'It's not, no, not the one...' you frown, as if in agony.

I retreat into my chair as the instrumental starts for the Pastoral bit. I swear you could have sung the Messiah alto part off by heart all the way through. You were always in a choir. Choral music, your greatest love. You even got me and Marion singing the Messiah with you when we were teenagers.

'What is this?' You poke at the cake.

'Just leave it!' I grab the plate and offer half the cake to Charlie, but he shakes his head and I eat it all to get rid of it.

'Mum, can I go for a walk on the common?' Charlie asks.

I feel the sinking of this afternoon, frazzled by it, left alone with it. But I'm not going to make Charlie sit out the full two hours. You barely realise he's here.

'Go on then, be back by five.'

'But, what about my children?' you cry as Charlie leaves.

One of your friends remarked that it's always about an hour into a visit that you start fretting about the children. Pretty much to order today.

'I'm your child, Mummy.'

'No, the younger ones, they need picking up, don't they?'

'They're with their mother, they're fine,' the usual refrain.

'But I'm sure we need to...they were on a train...'

'Everything's fine, there's nothing to worry about.' I try to smile in reassurance, wracking my brain for a change of subject.

You wriggle in your chair. 'I need to spend a penny.'

'Let me get someone.' Better for a member of staff to help you these days.

I'm back with Rosalie within a minute. I retreat, admiring as always Rosalie's patience and expertise in performing the ritual of getting you onto your frame to take the few painful steps to the en-suite, closing the door behind you. I pour myself the last of the stewed tea, wishing for something stronger. As the chorus piles in with Glory to God in the highest, I think how time was when I despised any church music. The claustrophobia of Anglican conformity bound up for me with the smell of Sunday dinner.

'But you sang in the church choir!' you would say. Yes, and you chose that for us, as you chose our piano lessons at age nine, second instrument at twelve. And you also took on Daddy's snobbishness about popular culture, severely restricting our access to any music outside the classical canon. But still music was the main thing you had outside of your immediate petty concerns. And I can see now that your controlling of us reflected the fundamental lack of control in your life: married to an ambitious public-school teacher, your Oxford degree reduced to dinner party conversation and a bit of part-time teaching. You used to say that you would choose being blind over being

deaf because you couldn't live without music. And now I
remember taking you to the Nine Lessons and Carols in the
cathedral one Christmas Eve when Charlie was little – my
first visit to a church in years. You whispered to me that the
choir was exceptional, and as they sang their performance
carols I was also moved by their exquisite singing, was
energised by their belting out the congregational standards.
I felt freed from the weight of churchgoing, able to
appreciate the music for its own sake.

Now I sit surrounded by the tokens of your life: the
picture I painted of the rooftops; the portrait of Mark by
his art student girlfriend; your mother's charcoals from
her sketching holidays. Photos of your family in its various
stages. The soprano soars with *Rejoice greatly O daughter
of Zion* and I am overwhelmed by the sinking void of
everything that was you. All the clichés about things to go.
I feel winded by the punch shock of its deserting you. The
soprano's Air, *And He shall speak peace unto the heathen*,
unbearable in its quiet delicacy.

'I don't know where, my daughter's...'

Rosalie guides you out of the en-suite; you are bent over
your frame, puffing exertion.

'Here she is, don't worry,' Rosalie steers you towards
me.

'Oh, I didn't know...' you cling onto the frame, your hat
hanging over the side of your face.

'It's all right, Mummy, sit down,' I say, irritation
replaced for now by an aching compassion. Rosalie coaxes
you into the chair, and immediately it's as though the effort
never happened. You give me that same bright smile as
when I arrived.

'I didn't know you were here.'

'I've been here all afternoon. I've been listening to the
music while you've been on the loo.'

You nod as the soprano sings *Come unto Him, all ye
that labour*. 'What is it?' The hat slips further, balanced on
the top of your glasses.

'It's the Messiah.' I get up to go to you.

Come unto Him that are heavy laden...

'Oh, did I give it to you?'

I take your hat and fold it away; smooth your hair as I turn to you.

and ye shall find rest unto your souls

'Yes, you did!' I say.

LEGACY

Legacy

by Rosie Cowan

'On your own?' There's a hopeful lilt, as if my solitary presence might signal I've jettisoned husband and kids in one fell swoop.

'Yep, David and the boys are busy with work and school.' They would have come, but I'm not putting them through this.

'Oh.' He shrinks back in the wheelchair, head wobbling on his scrawny turkey neck like one of those nodding dogs in the backs of cars.

'How are you?'

'Needn't think I'm leaving you a brass farthing. Sure, you never come near me.'

He's reiterated this at regular intervals for the past 17 years but it's gained resonance now. Not that an east Belfast end-of-terrace with red, white and blue kerb appeal is high on my wish list. The early Neolithic gable wall art, depicting the overzealous neighbourhood watch scheme, is unlikely to rival Banksy. We live in London. I ring him every few weeks, come over to visit once or twice a year. I stay with friends. The names Jake and Josh never pass his lips. His other grandchild, my brother Mark's 'bonny wee Robyn,' smiles out from a heart-shaped wooden frame on the bedside cabinet. She's got my unruly hair, poor kid. I place the small holdall on the bed and gently unzip it.

'Got you some joggers and PJs.'

'Don't need any. Brought a caseful from home. Gillian's bringing a goody box. They'd have had me but I wouldn't give them the bother.'

I booked him in here when the consultant spelt out the prognosis. Not that those two had any notion of having him. Mark's as much use as a chocolate teapot and Gillian's his airy-fairy soulmate. Her 'goody box' will probably consist of cake and sweets. Just the thing for a diabetic with throat cancer.

'You're in the best place now, Dad.'

I start unpacking into the flimsy chest of drawers. A dozen pairs of absorbent underpants, four pairs of pyjamas, four sets of brushed cotton tops and elasticated jogging bottoms. The top drawer is half empty. Squashed to one side are some ancient vests and greying Y-fronts, a couple of pairs of threadbare socks and a pristine white shirt, still in its plastic casing. He'll not take that collar size again.

'Are you eating? What did you have for lunch?'

'Foreign muck with noodles. Didn't touch it.'

Same old Dad who demanded a fish supper with such vehemence on his sole visit to a Chinese restaurant during my childhood that the waiter crossed the road to the chippy. Then he made a great show of wafting away our chow mein and chop suey aromas. Hardly surprising him not going full Ken Hom now.

'I'll ask if they can get you anything else, keep up your strength up.'

'I'm fine. Just the aul' legs playing silly beggars.'

He spits it out as if the recalcitrant limbs are rebelling on purpose. Just like he was sure I was when I told him about David.

***

'Of all the boys you must have spied at yon grand university of yours, you had to set your cap at thon. If he was Roman Catholic, at least he'd be white. You're doing this to spite us. Your mother's heart's clean broke.'

It wasn't the moment to bring up the Spanish conquest of the Americas, nor the Inquisition. Any new friend I made was routinely subjected to the latter, full name, address, school, sporting activities, whether they pronounced the eighth letter of the alphabet "aitch"' or '"haitch". God forbid religion be mentioned. A Dublin-born interloper christened Erin laboured under an ominous green cloud of suspicion for weeks till she outed herself as Church of Ireland. Even then...

Mum didn't look particularly heartbroken, just embarrassed. She never stood up to him. Always my fault for setting his nerves off. The Troubles had left him highly strung, like a badly tuned piano. Occasionally, she played the social conditioning card.

'He can't help it, love. He's just of his time.'

'Pity he votes in mine.'

Dad launched a last-ditch appeal to shop local. 'Don't know why you can't meet one of your own. Our Mark didn't go far.'

Could have taken my pick of an entire flute band. Gillian was brought up three streets away. If there'd been a home delivery option, Mark would have ticked it. I hadn't set my cap at David initially. An elegant giant strayed into my swim lane. A mean front crawl and a hot mess on the dancefloor, he failed miserably at racial profiling, won me over with funny stories. Strangely, his banter reminded me of Dad. When he wasn't pontificating in the style of the Very Reverend Doctor Ian Paisley, Dad was famed for blistering one-liners. Dished them out, couldn't take them. Went off on one when an English fella called him a Paddy.

'British as you are, don't you forget it.'

'You're all Paddies to us, mate. We don't discriminate.'

Dad was brilliant when I was wee. I loved our Saturday morning jaunts to the sweet shop, me dithering an age over strawberry or lemon bonbons. Took us to football most weeks. I didn't share his devotion to the local team but the craic was mighty, his running commentary hilarious. Genius at fixing things too.

'Oh leave it, Samuel, she hasn't ridden that bike in months,' said Mum, as a gearbox leaked grease on the paper spread across the kitchen table.

Better than reading it. The news wound him up like a

clockwork toy. Terrorists, politicians, bad as each other. Bloody Fee... - 'Samuel!' - Roman Catholics at it like rabbits, taking over like the blacks in South Africa. Fairies prancing about openly, no shame. More chance of the wardrobe opening up to Narnia than encountering anyone black round our way back then. Though I made several late-night expeditions in hopes of catching a stray Roman rabbit or fairy. By big school, I'd pledged my allegiance to feminism, anti-apartheid, civil rights. Read everything I could, aided and abetted by a history teacher who'd somehow evaded the head's draconian vetting system. Dad's rants seemed increasingly ridiculous. He'd swapped classroom for shipyard at 15 and revelled in his school of hard knocks status. Prided himself on being teetotal, never losing control, but his mind was a clenched fist, always spoiling for a fight.

'Dad, it's their country. We invaded it, slaughtered thousands, stole their gold and diamonds.'

'But this necklacing, setting fire to people. Savages.'

'And the Shankill Butchers weren't?'

***

The door swings open and a tiny woman in turquoise scrubs bustles in, bearing a tray. Possibly southeast Asian heritage, shy smile, broad Belfast accent. 'Well, Samuel, how you doing today? Didn't finish your wee lunch, did ye?'

'Didn't feel up to it, sorry, Christina.' Christina indeed.

'Aw, you must be starving. Wee cup of tea, you too, pet,' - she nods warmly in my direction – 'and a wee fruit scone. Rice pudding for you, Samuel?'

'Thanks, Christina, you're awful good to me.' Nice as ninepence. Though she's serving tea, not marrying me.

'You look a bit flushed, Dad. I'll take this off, shall I?' The room is stifling.

'Don't fuss me.'

But he doesn't resist when I feel his slightly clammy

forehead and manoeuvre him out of his cardigan. As I tug off the second sleeve, brittle twigs of fingers in crepe paper skin grasp my wrist.

'Too skinny. Still working all hours?'

'No, I've cut back a bit for now, so I can pop over more often.'

He holds my gaze, eyes boring into mine as he registers my meaning. Finally, he looks down, drops my arm.

***

I wrestled with it back then, my big decision. Split up for a few months after uni, not that I ever told anyone at home. Felt like I'd wrenched out my own heart and stamped on it. Thanks be, David kept the faith. Even now I can't bear to think I could have lost him. Dad would probably have danced in the street.

'I just reckon they should stay in their own country.'

'Bit difficult when your ancestors are kidnapped and shipped halfway round the world.'

'Ach, that's all past. They can go home anytime now.'

'After 400 years in the Caribbean and 40 in England? Not like the neighbours are still watering the plants.'

Undaunted by my bleak forecast, David wanted to meet my parents. Dad promised to be on his best behaviour, only because he saw a chance to reason with David, his definitions of best behaviour and reason being somewhat flexible. Mark developed a crucial summit at his in-laws'. I'd hoped for a brief drop-in, but Mum insisted on a roast with all the trimmings.

'I hope you like our traditional Sunday dinner.' Every syllable enunciated like she was auditioning to read the news.

'Very tasty, Mrs McCullough.'

Dad was uncharacteristically quiet at first. He seemed wrong-footed by David's friendliness, but normal service soon resumed.

LEGACY

'Muir, that's a Scottish surname.'

'Lots of the Jamaican plantation owners were Scottish.' Dad looked bewildered.

'Slaves took their masters' surnames.'

'Oh, I...I see. But your people came to London?'

'In 1958, ten years after the Windrush. Crystal Palace ever since.'

Dad seized his opportunity when I was helping Mum clear the table for pudding. From the kitchen, I caught '...nothing at all personal against you, son, you understand... just not the natural order of things...I'm sure your parents would prefer one of your own...'

'My parents love Grace and so do I.'

I wanted to hurl the trifle in Dad's face, but David, mindful of Mum's feelings and culinary efforts, kept his customary cool. We forced down custard, mandarin jelly and sponge fingers like an Orange parade through Ardoyne, made our excuses and left. Dad never quite closed the door afterwards, but it wasn't really open either. If I hadn't gone back, it would have slammed shut forever. David's parents were always delighted when we called by. Winnie would fire rapid patois at me through a broad grin while Abigay supplied everyone with mountains of plantain, jerk chicken and rice. I even went to church with Abigay a few times, Baptist, Dad would have loved the hymns. I'd written off Dad's supreme deity as a narcissistic misogynist with homicidal tendencies. Abigay's chap, on the other hand, seemed sound. One evening while David was out with Winnie, I found myself pouring my woes onto her generous shoulders.

'Don't worry, my love, we're your family now.'

We got married in Jamaica. It was a great excuse for Winnie and Abigay to reconnect with long-lost relatives and easier to explain away missing persons.

'My folks just aren't good with heat and long flights. We're planning a party in Belfast soon.' Abigay shot me a sympathetic look. She was wonderful when the twins arrived, though Mum did her fair share. Made a big fuss of them when she came over, took lots of photos 'for your father.' I brought the boys to Belfast a few times to see her. Dad would say hello and then head out to 'give us all space,' but there's no fooling kids.

'Why does Granda not like us?'

'Granda's not well. He can't take a lot of excitement.'

'Is that why he's so cross? I'd be very cross if I couldn't be exciting.'

'But Granny, Grandpa Winnie says there's a law he has to give big hugs every time he sees us, and he's got a tricky heart.'

Mum's health gave out first though, a massive stroke. David and I left the boys with Winnie and Abigay and headed over. Five long days and nights in intensive care, then a merciful passing. Dad was utterly distraught. Howled like a man possessed during the funeral service, almost stumbled into the grave. Afterwards, he slumped in his armchair, staring at the empty seat opposite. First time I ever felt sorry for him. It wasn't just practical reliance, he was always able to fend for himself, but he'd loved her with every fibre of his being. The twinkle in his eyes had been switched off. In the early days of his grief, David and I were just vague shapes, handing him endless cups of tea and slices of toast he hardly touched. His old anger seemed to be ebbing away and I let myself believe his pain might soften the ground for a seed to grow. Within the year, however, he'd turned his back on the road to Damascus.

'David and I were thinking of popping over a weekend next month. We could bring the boys if you felt up to it?'

'Can you not just come on your own, love? I can't be doing with strangers now.'

***

Mid-morning, he's propped up on pillows in bed, still in his pyjamas, steel wires of bristle poking through his chin, a state of affairs he'd never have tolerated previously. I've brought the weekend sports supplements, safer than the news sections. He carefully sets them aside for later, on top of Friday's *Guardian*, definitely not his preferred reading. One of the staff must have left it. We drink tea, chat about the shipyard and old neighbours, lapse into companionable silence in front of the football. After a couple of hours, I stand up to go.

'Grace...' His voice is low, wavery, but there's a note of urgency. I turn the television down, bend closer...'Why did you marry him?'

I lurch backwards, overturning the chair, just about manage to right it before dashing from the room. The corridor blurs and stings with hot tears.

'Are you okay, pet?' A petite form in sky blue swims into view, Christina. 'Not easy, watching your poor daddy suffer.' I don't trust myself to do more than nod. She has no idea. Perhaps she does. He's probably not the only well-mannered bigot she's encountered.

Back at Erin's, I'm torn. Seeing him again feels like betraying David and the boys. But he's a sick, lonely old man with a son who scarcely utters a word to him and a daughter-in-law whose singsong cheeriness sets my teeth on edge. Gillian's stopped Robyn visiting, figures it's too much for her, what with her GCSEs. Dad's convinced she popped in last week, but he's getting confused.

'Look, you've no obligation to the aul' fecker,' - I love the way Erin's Dub accent massages swear words into terms of endearment, the perfect antidote to Dad's habit of injecting entirely innocent vocabulary with venom - 'but it's your decision, nobody else's. Do what you can square in your own heart. Maybe give yourself a break and come back when...'

***

He's refused further treatment and for once I agree with him. The consultant says it would cause distress and only prolong the inevitable. He's lying down, shrivelled and pale, a ghost faded into the sheets. I sit on the bed and he reaches out, hands shaking as I stroke them, his eyes welling up with uncharted oceans. His breath is laboured, then, a rasping whisper...'My bonny...bonny Grace...'

***

He's sliding in and out, a diver venturing new depths, yet yearning to surface again. The fluids drip is gone, only the pain relief pump remains. On his bedside cabinet sit metal containers of ice chips and glycerine swabs to wet his lips. I trace a soft greeting on his forehead and say hello, hearing and touch are the last senses to linger. He shifts and murmurs. His breathing undulates in ragged staccato code I can't decipher. Nurses come and go, checking him, asking if I need anything. Daylight dwindles into dusk, a luminous disc of moon pierces faded floral curtains. I lean back in the chair... My eyes twitch and jerk open, while. Gradually, I become aware of a new stillness. I am alone. I stand up and look down on the familiar face of a stranger. He's slipped through my grasp once more, one final time.

***

We bury him on a bitterly cold day in March. The service is short, more homily than eulogy. I read a lesson, Robyn reads a poem, James Baldwin's 'Paradise,' an unusual choice, for Dad or a funeral, but it works.

'Picked it herself,' Gillian smugly informs me.

Praise be, Gillian inclines more toward Hallmark than Heaney. Robyn's voice is halting, emotional, yet she is clear and feisty as her namesake. He left her the house in trust. I'm hurt for Jake and Josh, though I don't begrudge her, she's a really nice kid, considering.

***

Afterwards, she's alone, perched on the edge of the church hall stage, long skinny legs in black woolly tights, heels drumming against the wooden platform, dark mass of curls sweeping her shoulders. I leave David with Erin and head over.

'You read well. Interesting poem.'

'Thanks, not sure Granda would've heard of him but I like his stuff. How's Jake and Josh? Been a few years since I seen them.'

'Must be. They'll be 15 in August, nearly as tall as David. All grown up like yourself. How's the revision?'

'Not bad, I need good grades to do A levels, get to uni.'

'What do you want to study?'

'Not sure, maybe law, like you, human rights and that.'

'You've a great law school on your doorstep.'

'I know, but...' – she rolls her eyes in the direction of her parents – 'might be good to move away... Actually, I want to ask your advice about Granda's house sometime. I won't get it till I'm 18 but selling it would pay for uni, if I get in...'

I take a step back and look at her. That glorious teenage girl fusion of supreme confidence and awkward angst reminds me of someone.

'Well, how about this summer, after your exams, you come stay with us for a bit? Get to know Jake and Josh better, explore London, maybe look round a few unis?'

'Aw, I'd love to, Aunt Grace, that'd be pure class.'

My Gam Speaks in Remnants

by Elizabeth M. Castillo

My Gam says my friends Ibrahim and Mehdi
ne sont pas des gens à fréquenter. Remnants of
some unfounded fear of the unknown, of the veiled
neighbour
and their mysterious prayer calls creaking out
over the quasi-silence of the pre-dawn. She slaps
my wrist when I ask her *ki dir, mo Gam? Ki posizion?*
Pas de créole à table! Or "Patois" as she calls it.
Ce n'est pas la langue des gens bien!
Remnants of "simpler" times, when things spoken coloured
the world, our tiny island, in black and white. *Un langage*
vulgaire!
she calls it, and the words sound like vomit in her mouth,
more than in mine. She is the reason I was never taught;
the reason people squint and cock their head
when I order fruit in the market, or faratha in the street.
Français, c'est mieux! Le vrai français!
Sharp-edged remnants of colonial caprice, smacking
of self-loathing. And yet, as the end creeps upon her,
it's the "vulgar" patois we speak, when she tells me stories
of my grandfather *ki ti ene zom; ene papa; ene mari; oh!*
Il était tout pour moi! and those
malabar girls, who looked just like her,
but without my Gam's greatest pride- her distinguishing
feature
(besides jet-black hair, like a waist-length waterfall):
her God-given pair of the brightest, bluest eyes.

FLOWERS FOR MISS HAVISHAM

Flowers for Miss Havisham

by Wendy Sacks Jones

The flower market was about to close. Some of the stallholders were starting to load the unsold bunches back into their vans, water from emptied buckets trickled along the street gutters and broken daffodil blooms coloured the pavement. Anisha bent down to pick up the head of one, still perfect but amputated from its stem, and then dropped it in the flow of gutter water where it would be safe from people's feet. Daffodils. The best flowers ever. Honest, easy flowers. Their proper name was narcissus, but daffodil suited them so much better. Daff-o-dil. Just the sound of the word made you smile, however bad your problems. She liked the pale buttery ones with apricot centres the most. It was as if God or evolution — she was no longer sure what she believed in – had opened the paintbox and mixed varying blobs of yellow, orange, white and green as an experiment. God – or the other thing – was showing off.

At home the back garden was full of daffodils. Her dad grew them, the boring regular ones, yellow in the middle and yellow around the outside. They'd be in bloom soon and her mum would have jugs of them all over the house. The odd thing was they didn't smell that good – Anisha once told her mum they had a pong like cat wee and her mum said that wasn't a polite thing to say.

Her mum had no sense of humour. But there had to be some daffodils with lovely scents, surely. The flower-breeders would grow them that way so people would want to buy them. They were clever – that was science rather than God or even evolution. The market had its own special smell – sweet and flowery of course, but with a hint of fried onions and kebabs and in places a stink of something rotten. It came in waves as you walked through different parts of the market and if you closed your eyes, you knew exactly which part you were in. She really preferred the market in the morning.

If she had time, she'd walk through on her way to school when the flowers were fresh and the stall-holders hopeful, cracking early morning jokes with each other and wrapping their hands round scalding mugs of tea. There was one woman who always smiled at her, a cheerful, slightly sweary woman with hair as orange as some of the daffodil centres. Anisha sometimes dreamed of getting a Saturday job there. She couldn't imagine anything better than selling flowers. The woman would teach her how to display them in the buckets and how to persuade people to buy an extra bunch. But there was no point in even thinking about it. She wouldn't be allowed.

She walked on. It was nearly half past four now and she needed to get home, or there'd be a fuss again. A few of the stallholders were hanging on, trying to squeeze the last bit of business out of the day. The man on the stall next to the coffee shop was calling out, 'Two bunches of beautiful roses for a quid. C'mon on you lovely people, I'm giving them away.' The people at the market were smart and funny. It was like stand-up, they could be on TV. But noone else was taking much notice now and she was sorry for the man and his roses. Once wilted, flowers had no value, and these already looked limp. Yet two for a pound was tempting. Roses were more sophisticated than daffodils. They were flowers that thought a lot of themselves. And they were usually pricey. She hovered and the stallholder turned to her.

'Here you go, my lovely. Roses for an English rose.'

She adjusted her hijab, pretended still to be considering the purchase and then fumbled in her purse for a pound coin. The English rose thing, the man was probably joking, she couldn't be sure. But it was better than the things she sometimes got called. Perhaps it was irony. She'd been doing irony in English and it was complicated.

'Hi,' said Jag.

'Oh, hi.'

Her cheeks tingled. Where had he come from? He was standing there, right next to her. Flower markets couldn't be Jag's thing. He must have followed her from school. She handed over the coin, settled the crimson roses in the crook of her arm and heaved her schoolbag back onto her shoulder. She looked up at Jag for a second – his eyelashes were longer and blacker than she remembered and she wanted to touch them, to feel them tickling her finger. Please God, let him think of something to say first.

'Who you buying those for then?' he asked.

'Noone. Just to take home.'

'Nice. Fancy a coffee?'

'I don't drink coffee. Remember?'

'Or an ice cream? There's a place over there. I'll pay.'

Jag was a mate of her brother's, 17 and fit and Sikh and forbidden. Their friendship had been the best week of her life. They'd walked and talked and told each other their dreams and once, just once, she'd let him kiss her and thought she might die mid-kiss. But then her sister had found out and told her parents. Her mum had screamed, 'How could you?' over and over again. She didn't seem to want an answer, although Anisha could have given her one, and then when she'd calmed down a bit, she'd said, 'You're not to see him again. Not ever. Do you understand?'

Her dad was worse. He hadn't shouted, but had just shaken his head and said, 'I'm so disappointed in you, Anisha,' in that soft, reasonable voice of his. And all she had said was,

'We didn't do it, if that's what you're worried about.'

Then her mother had lost it all over again and yelled,

'Oh my God, is this my daughter?' and started that pretend-crying she did when she wanted everyone to know

68

how much she was suffering.

That was one of the worst things about her mother, always trying to make everyone else feel guilty. Anisha would never behave like that when she had kids. She ran to her room and slammed the door and looked for a bag to pack. She found one, but of course she didn't pack it and she didn't run away. She wouldn't have known where to run to. She'd have been too scared to run away with Jag and anyway, when she texted him to tell him that her parents were monsters, he just laughed. She wasn't sure what she'd have done if he had suggested running away. But now everything was quiet again in the house and she was on probation. That's what her dad had said. Proving that she could be trusted.

'I can't, Jag. You know I can't.'

'It's just an ice cream. Aw, Nish, come on.'

'Don't call me that. My dad would kill me if he thought I'd even spoken to you.'

Her dad would never kill her. Her mum might, maybe, but not her dad. But it was what people said, a way of describing something really dreadful that just wasn't worth risking.

'Oh well, please yourself.' He stepped back a pace and looked over her shoulder, as if he'd forgotten she was there.

She had to say something, she couldn't just leave it at that, but she couldn't think of anything that wouldn't make things worse. There were some situations that were so bad they didn't have solutions. She rubbed a finger along the stem of one of the roses and felt a tiny prick. Idiot. Roses had thorns. You didn't stroke them. A small bubble of blood emerged near the tip of her finger, a perfect sphere, exactly the colour of the roses, and she hoped Jag hadn't noticed. She shifted the flowers to her other arm, wiped her finger on the side of her blazer and kept it pressed there. The blazer was maroon, the blood wouldn't show.

'I'm sorry, Jag.'

He turned back to her and smiled, a hard smile that

wasn't really a smile at all.

'No problem. See you around then.' And he was gone.

The man who'd sold her the roses was eying her and grinning.

'Never mind, darling. Plenty more fish in the sea. Lovely girl like you shouldn't have no problems there.'

She put her back on him and looked at her one pound roses. Stupid man. Stupid flowers. She shouldn't have bought them. Daffodils would have been better. Or tulips, or carnations, or anything really. The roses were still buds, scentless and picked before their time, tightly wrapped in their deep red petals, wrinkled before they could open, enclosing secrets that would now never be revealed. They reminded her of that character in the book they were doing for GCSE. Estella's guardian. Wrinkles and secrets.

Miss... Miss Havisham, that was it.

One lesson they'd watched part of an old film and there was this scene with Miss Havisham where she had loads of dead flowers on her dressing table. The actress who played her was beautiful, even if she was very old. She had her head covered too, though the material was flimsy and see-through, and her hair, all yellow-grey and wispy, definitely wasn't hidden. But it was the flowers Anisha remembered most.

Roses, red roses.

Miss Havisham had never bothered to throw them away after her boyfriend hadn't turned up for the wedding. Well, she could have this lot too. Flowers for Miss Havisham, that's what they were. Anisha hadn't contributed much in the class discussion after the film. She just sat there trying to imagine what it was like to be so badly let down that you never left your room again and hated men forever. The other kids said Miss Havisham was weird and no-one would really behave like that and Dickens was boring, but they were wrong. She was the saddest character in any book Anisha had ever read and she loved her for that sadness. All cobwebs and veils and dead roses and disappointment.

She walked on, looking for a waste bin, while all around her the stalls were being dismantled.

The Way We Are

by Ben Stevenson

ความเมตตา ~ KINDNESS
20. 03. 19

Dawn in Bangkok had begun to cast its amber rays over the city streets as Non returned from her morning run. She picked up two coffees from the street vendor outside her building and took them upstairs. The injured stranger was in the kitchen, listening to the radio. Her foreign guest had dressed his wounds and looked better. He greeted Non with a wounded smile as she handed him one of the coffee cups. She booked him a taxi home while they sipped their coffees and chatted in perfect English until his driver arrived.

They exchanged numbers and Non waved him off from her second-floor window, before going about her day.Her boss from the agency called her landline at midday. He was angry. A chorus of expletives that made their way across the airwaves conveyed his feelings towards Non's no-show at her clients last night. She tried to explain the unforeseen circumstances, but without much luck. He aggressively warned her she was on her last chance, before hanging up. As Non put down the phone, an automated voice notified her that she had two unread voicemail messages. She pressed play.

'Friday, 4.20 pm. "Hello, Non. It is Samorn calling from Dr Wattanawong's office at Yanhee Hospital. This is confirmation of your consultation to see—"'Samorn's voice tailed off as Non made a note in her diary and skipped to the next message.

'Next new voicemail: Friday 5.12 pm. "Darling, Non, it is your mother. Please call back so we can speak. Your father is just very traditional. He does not want to lose you, but he says if you go through with this...thing... well... he cannot accept it. I know he is very set in his ways but do please listen to him. It is for the best of the family. Please call us when you get this.'"

A single tear began to roll down Non's cheek. Feeling lightheaded, she headed onto her balcony to clear her head and get some air. Taking a deep breath, she stared into the concrete jungle as the war inside her raged on between her head and her heart.

มิตรภาพ ~ FRIENDSHIP
17. 05. 19

A grey smog cloaked Krung Thep. The City of Angels, however, was alive. Vivid neon signs illuminated the cityscape. Relentless traffic suffocated the motorways. Students and tourists flooded the red-light districts. Soi dogs prowled the quiet back streets, howling at the hidden moon. William Taylor was smoking, listening to music on his balcony. The Englishman lived in a plush 34th floor condo in Bang Rak, facing the river. From his vantage point, he could only just make out the long tail boats in the distance, chugging along the murky waters of the Chao Phraya. He was alone.

His wife, Sarai, had taken the children again. They spent a lot of time away from home these days. Usually, this was at Sarai's family home in Buriram, a remote town in Isaan, 410 kilometres north-east of the capital. William was not in favour of the arrangement. Neither was he opposed to the arrangement. Instead, he was numb to it. The truth was he and his wife had been growing apart for some time. For their recent wedding anniversary, Sarai took the kids to her sister's flat in Phaya Thai and stayed the night. William drank half a bottle of scotch in front of the TV, before heading to Sukhumvit and shooting pool late into the night with fellow strangers - disenfranchised drunks. He loved his kids deeply and he loved Sarai, but as the mother of his children, not as his wife.

After coming around from his brief trance, he glanced at his counterfeit watch. He had ten minutes before he needed to leave. Calculating time, he plucked out a final beer from the fridge and turned off the stereo, instead preferring to spend his final few minutes at home drinking in the symphony of noise from the urban metropolis below. Silom Road was bristling with early evening activity as he made his way towards *Sala Daeng* BTS station. As he walked, an eclectic mix of Thai street food aromatics and petrol fumes filled his lungs.

He had arranged to meet Non at Nana Plaza and even though he was running late, he still decided to take a detour to Patpong night market for a short therapy visit. Eventually, he caught the Skytrain towards *Siam*, changing lines there before finally disembarking at Nana and heading west, towards the vibrant playground of bars, restaurants, and hotels that formed the plaza.

Non was waiting at the plaza entrance. She was dressed in a sequinned black mini dress that barely stretched beyond her narrow hips and modest heels that took her up to his height. Her appearance had changed in the two months since the last and only time they had previously met. Her hair was longer and lighter than before. Her lips, coated in dark red paint, were fuller, and her chest visibly more ample than he remembered. The pair exchanged a customary *wai* and some awkward pleasantries over a cigarette before heading on towards their chosen haunt.

Markitiny Noodle Bar was nestled above a franchise American sports bar on Sukhumvit 4 Alley. It was modest, with fraying decor and worn stools surrounding a square island bar in the centre of the room. On William's recommendation they settled at two free stools on the near side, adjacent to a wall plastered with polaroid pictures of backpackers and tourists.

'What are we drinking?' Non asked as she draped her clutch bag over the back of her stool.

'Something cold and alcoholic,' William replied. 'I'm

going to need it.'

'Beer?'

'Yes. Let's get a bucket.'

'Okay. And to eat?'

'Mee Krob.'

'I'll join you.'

Non delivered their order in Thai to the man behind the bar who then nonchalantly filled a bucket with ice and placed inside eight large green bottles. He rested the bucket on a stand between their stools and handed them two damp beer mats before returning to the bar to prepare their noodles. There was a silence as both reached for their first beer, mutually hoping to dispel the awkwardness in the air. William began hastily swigging his Chang, so eventually it was Non who broke the ice.

'You look much better than the last time I saw you.'

He made a downward gaze, uncomfortably picking at the sticker on his beer bottle. It was unfathomably true. The last and only time the two had met in person, William had been in a seriously bad way. He had been mugged and beaten in a side alley just behind Soi Cowboy after another night of heavy drinking. That night, he had lost his phone, wallet and, devastatingly, his late father's *Omega Seamaster 300* watch. The latter was a family heirloom handed to him on his 21st birthday and was irreplaceable. Non had encountered him in the aftermath on her way between clients. Finding him bruised, bloodied and confused, she did not think twice about helping him to her small flat around the corner in Watthana, cancelling her remaining outcalls that night and letting him crash on her small single bed while she slept on the floor. William never forgot her kindness to a stranger that night and they had kept in touch via WhatsApp ever since.

'Thanks, I guess.' he said, smiling bashfully to disguise his malaise.

They both drank their beer.By the time their noodles arrived, William had just come back from another cigarette outside. He and Non were already on their third Chang. They discussed William's family, Non's job and the city they called home. Empty stomachs meant they were feeling slightly tipsy and so the sweet and sour Mee Krob was a welcome sight to both.

'How old are your children?' Non asked, as she tore open the wrapping paper of her disposable chopsticks and tucked into her noodles.

'Four and six. They've grown so quickly.'

'Can you show me a picture?

'Sure.'

William flicked through the gallery on his mobile. He stopped on a picture from last year showing him walking through Lumphini Park with his children. His younger daughter sat on his shoulders as her elder brother skipped alongside him, holding his hand. It felt like a lifetime ago.

'So cute!' Non said. 'What are their names?'

'Leo and Amara.'

'They are lovely names. You look like a great father.'

Her face struggled to disguise her anguish as she spoke and William picked up on it.

'You look upset, Non. Have I done something?'

'Not at all. That picture just reminds me of how my father and I used to be.'

'Used to be?'

'He doesn't accept me anymore.' She paused and took a breath. 'Ever since I became *Phuying*, my father has stopped my family from seeing me. I have dishonoured him.'

It was a bolt from the blue. *Phuying* was a common term that ladyboys used when referring to themselves. William tried not to let his astonishment register on his face.

'I'm so sorry, Non,' he said, still bewildered at the revelation she had previously been a man.

He remained steadfast and pulled her into a comforting embrace.

'It's okay. I know exactly how you feel.'

Returning to his stool, William pushed his half-eaten Mee Krob away. He had lost his appetite. Non had already done the same with hers.

'I never told my father my biggest secret because I was too scared. My worst fear was that I would lose him.'

Non stayed quiet. Her brow furrowed at the suggestion that there was more to William Taylor than met the eye. There was a pause that seemed to last forever. Then William broke his silence.

'I'm a gay man.' he said, on cue. Shock spread across his face as his brain raced to grapple with the words that had just come out of his mouth. 'I've never said those words to anyone before.' He looked almightily relieved. 'I'm gay,' he said again. Non looked perplexed.

'But your family?' she said. 'Your wife?'

'I have genuinely never told a soul,' William said. 'My wife may have her suspicions. But I don't think she even cares. She's probably too occupied with secret lovers anyway.'

'Why are you telling me first?' Non said.

'I thought we shared similar sentiments about our fathers.'

William's divulgence certainly seemed to cheer up Non.

'I think we should celebrate.' she said, on a whim. 'Come with me. I want us to have some fun tonight!'

They paid the bill and made their way out of Nana Plaza. Non hailed a passing tuk-tuk. The driver pulled over sharply. He hopped out and introduced himself as Pranut, before eagerly escorting them both inside.

'Never been in one of these before,' William said.

'Tonight, there is a first time for everything!'

The tuk-tuk motored away and joined a sea of madness. Decrepit vehicles, rusty scooters and overstuffed people carriers roared past each other as if they were racing. Plumes of toxic black smoke filled the stifling Bangkok air. William and Non hung on for dear life as Pranut navigated the city streets at what seemed like breakneck speed. Eventually, they were afforded a respite as he hit traffic and began inching towards a busy intersection, beeping his horn and cutting off motorcyclists trying to edge ahead. William used the opportunity to ask the question on his mind.

'Where are you taking me, Non?'

'Soon. You will find out soon.' She replied, as the sputtering, three-wheeled motor skidded away.

ความทุกข์ ~ SORROW
23. 05. 19

William savoured the rarity of being stood on an empty Skytrain as he made his way to Non's place. The Bangkok weather was playing tricks again. Blue skies and golden sunshine had radiated Bang Rak as he'd left his condo just a few minutes ago, yet as William neared Watthana, the skies darkened abruptly, and a deluge of rainfall began to fall, its pellets dancing ferociously atop the empty carriage. He was conflicted. Sarai had called the previous evening to say she was coming back and she was bringing Leo and Amara with her. They were due to arrive home in a few hours. He had no idea how he would tell them. In fact, a nagging voice in the back of his head was still unsure whether he would even tell them at all.

He desperately needed to speak to Non. Invariably, William hoped she again would provide him with a voice of reason. He had called her immediately after putting the phone down to Sarai, but she did not pick up. He had sent voice notes this morning too, asking to meet. No response. Presumably, she was hard pressed at work and William didn't think it would be acceptable to answer the phone when with a client. Undeterred, he had decided to head to her flat anyway, hoping to catch her on the way back in from a busy night. As the Skytrain rolled through *Asok* BTS station, the penultimate stop, William cast his mind back six days to the last time he had seen Non. It had been a blissful, euphoric night.

Pranut had ferried them around the city, as they hopped from one gay bar to another, soaking up the LGBT scene and dancing the night away. With the help of Non, and a copious amount of *Sangsom*, William had let loose, and even got the number of a Dutch expat he had spent some time flirting with. He smiled to himself, excited to reminisce on the night with Non and gossip about the stories and laughs.

William tried calling Non once more when he reached the front of her building, but to no avail, so he decided to shelter under the doorway and wait. He was about to light his third cigarette in a row when an elderly male neighbour eventually let him into the building on his way back from some morning errands. He climbed briskly to the second floor and knocked vehemently on Non's door. Nobody answered the knock.

'Non?' William called out.

Nobody answered the call. William pressed his face against the door. Distinctly, he could hear the murmurs of a TV reverberating in the background. If she wasn't home, he thought, then why was it on? Growing concerned, William began to look for a spare key somewhere nearby. He checked under the doormat outside the door. Nothing.

He checked her post-box.

Nothing again.

In despair, he leaned out of the staircase window. On the far side of the wet windowsill lay a small plant pot. It looked strangely out of place there. Without thinking, William picked it up. He was greeted by the sight of a small silver key. Without celebrating his luck, he raced back to Non's entrance and tried it. The key slid into the lock seamlessly and the door opened.

'Non?' William called out again as he entered.

The apartment was comprised of a modest open plan kitchen diner, and a single en-suite situated towards the back. Non was not in the main room. William turned the TV off on his way into the bedroom, where the sight before him made his heart jump into his throat. Non was lain out over her bed, motionless. Her skin was a pallid white, marbled by a blotchy crimson pattern mapping her veins. Various empty pill bottles lay open on the floor. William felt like he had been sucker punched. He fell to his knees, broke down and wept. After several minutes, he tried to gather his emotions. Through tear-glazed eyes, he shut his late friend's eyelids with his fingertips and pulled the duvet over her to cover her modesty. As he was doing so, out of the corner of his eye he noticed a small piece of yellow paper neatly folded into four curled up in her hand.

It was a note.

Some sixth sense told him to open it. After deliberation, he carefully unravelled it and read:

For my newest friend William,
Be true to yourself, even if I could not.
Don't be afraid.
We are the way we are.

Even in death, Non had provided him with a voice of kindness and friendship he had rarely experienced in his adult life. And in that moment, his mind was made up. He made her a promise.

STRING THEORY

String Theory
by Richard Smith

I bought the first dog way back, soon after my wife left me.
I probably shouldn't have, because I don't much like dogs.
They smell and they eat roadkill, and they will crap just
about anywhere, but I suppose it was company of sorts.
Mainly I bought it because it was somebody else's idea - a
woman of course – so it was too much effort not to buy it,
at the time. I do a lot of things because it's too much effort
not to, especially when there's a woman involved. Getting
married, for example, or going to the maternity unit to
watch my son being born. You'd think things like that
would be easier not to do, but life has taught me that no,
just do the stuff people expect you to, or that they want you
to, and it's usually a lot less effort.

Harry was very different to me in that respect. Harry
never did anything he didn't want to do, and that made
things quite difficult between us. I met Harry again a short
while ago when I was out with my dog. Oddly enough, the
reason getting a dog was suggested in the first place, is the
reason I always said I wouldn't have one, and that's because
dogs need walking. According to the woman who was giving
me counselling back then, having a dog would get me out
into the fresh air, a real tonic for depression.

Technically, I don't think I was ever depressed, I was just
unhappy with the way life had turned out for me, and I was
quite angry about things to tell the truth. If I'd had anything
about me, I would have stopped going to the counselling
after a couple of sessions anyway. I knew they weren't
doing much to improve my state of mind; all that nonsense
about how we can all control our own lives, we all have
choices we can make, all that rubbish. Still, it was nice to
be with a woman who would sit and listen to me, and who

wasn't constantly telling me what an arse I was; not at first anyway, although we ended up having that conversation eventually. Also, she was very attractive, which made the sessions almost worth looking forward to.

We fell out in the end of course, that always seems to be the way; over the dog as it happens. When I told her I wished I'd never bought the stupid thing and I shouldn't have listened to her, she said, 'It was only a suggestion Frank.' That's what they do, they get you to do stuff and when it goes wrong, suddenly it's your fault.

'You told me to get the bloody dog.' I told her.

'It was a suggestion, to get you out and about, Frank. You made the decision to get the dog, and we've talked about your swearing in these sessions, haven't we? And we've talked about how you're in control of making your own decisions.'

'Jesus,' I said, 'this is exactly what my wife used to do.'

'I'm not your wife Frank, we've talked about that as well,' she said, 'I'm trying to help you.'

'Right.' I said.

And that was the last session I had. 40 quid for 40 minutes they cost me, a pound a minute. Christ. And then there's been all the dog food, and the vet's visits, and you can't just drive somewhere miles away and throw them out of the car anymore, because they're all bloody chipped. I mean, Jesus.

So anyway, a dog was the reason I saw Harry again after so long. Of course, it was a different dog by then, the first one died after about 12 years I think, but I'd gotten so used to picking up dog shit by then, that I went straight out and got another one. At least I think that's why I got another one. I've never been altogether sure why I do most of the things I do, except, as I say, it's usually easier to do something than not to do it. Maybe it was easier to keep having a dog around, than not to have one.

I was out walking the dog in the park when I saw him. He looked a lot older, but I knew it was him straight away,

I could feel the string pushing its way out of my chest pretty much as soon as I laid eyes on him, and in a matter of seconds there it was for me and Harry both to see. A piece of plain, brown, old fashioned string. I started simple, though my heart was banging like the clappers; I didn't want to scare him off. I sat down on the other end of the park bench he was on, and I said 'Good morning.'

'Good morning,' he said, leaning over and giving the string a little tug. Just a tweak for little bit of pain at first. He hadn't recognised me.

Then there was the usual silence. As a child, Harry had never liked a lot of conversation, and it seemed he hadn't changed in that respect. I tried to get a good look at him without being too obvious, and from what I could see, he was in good health, although still thin as a bean pole; thin face, thin legs, painfully thin fingers. I tried to remember exactly how long it had been since I'd seen him last, perhaps use it as a conversation opener, but for the life of me I couldn't pin it down.

I tried to add it up. I'd had the first dog for round about 12 years and I was sure that Harry had never seen it; and when I bumped into Harry in the park, I'd had the second one five years. Or was it six? That meant that I hadn't seen my son for around 17 or 18 years. That took me by surprise a little, I have to say. There's no wonder the string had all but disappeared; I'd pretty much forgotten about it. It wasn't always like that, and the last thing I want to do is give the impression that I'm a bad person who never cared about his own child. It's just that in Harry's case, unusually for me, it was easier all round not to do something, than do something, and by that I mean that it was much easier not to be around Harry than it was to be around him. In fact, the last time I'd seen Harry, shortly before I got the first dog, he'd stepped away from me, and pulling the string, he'd said,

'Fuck off, Frank.'

Not *Dad*, you'll notice, but *Frank*. So I did. Fuck off,

that is; because I'd had enough by then, of being sworn at, of being the butt of all the anger. That child was angry from the day he was born, and I never did understand where it came from. And there I was nearly 20 years later, on a park bench, trying to think of a way to 'un-fuck off' myself from my son. All I wanted to do, was think of something simple to say, and it wasn't coming very easily. Nothing came very easily where Harry was concerned. When he was born I did the expected thing and cried in the delivery room for a minute or so, although if I'd known what was coming my way, I would have cried a lot longer than I did.

I loved being a father at first. Ringing round the family to tell them it was a boy, how much he weighed, who he looked like. I mean, to me he looked like a tiny yellow gnome, but grandparents always like to hear who a baby looks like for some reason. Just checking the heritage, probably. Then there was the first little stuffed Tigger and the soft blue blanket that I bought him and had to take to the hospital, because the jaundice and his not feeding properly, kept him and his mother on the ward for four days. Four days of calm. Four days that I loved being a father.

Then they both came home. Jesus.

They say that time goes really quick when you have children. They say that you need to make the most of it because it will be gone in the blink of an eye. What *they* don't tell you is how long the years can feel when all your child does is scream and cry and pull at the string that's poking out of your chest. I thought that string was going to make me the best Dad in the world; I thought it was going to make me a new man; I thought for a while, *stupid old Frank*, that it was going to make his mother finally fall in love with me. I even hoped for a while, that it would make the one attached to my balls disappear; the one that had appeared on my wedding morning. Here I am years later, and it still makes my eyes water, remembering how Harry's mother used to have so much fun yanking on that one, until she finally met the woman of her dreams, and moved out.

Jesus. The pain they can give you.

What actually happened after Harry was born, was that he pulled that string from day one. The mystery to me was how hard he could pull, right from the start. He pulled it when we took him to the hospital for his MRI scans, and during every paediatrics appointment he ever had, and every time we got any of his medical test results, and eventually every time he called me Frank instead of Dad, he pulled it, but most of all, most of all, he pulled that string the hardest when they said, 'We're really sorry Mr and Mrs Preston, there's no doubt that your son's on the spectrum.' That's when Harry pulled on that string so hard it squashed my heart right up against the inside of my ribcage.

I mean, fuck. Jesus, fuck. A man could drown in that sort of pain.

Truthfully, I nearly did drown, which is why, when I went to pick up Harry from his mother's that day, when he looked at me like I was a complete stranger, and said 'Fuck off Frank,' I did just that. And I never went back. And I didn't see Harry from that day, until the other day in the park almost two decades later. And that didn't go well either. Because I asked him, 'How's your mother, Harry?' and he said,

'What the fuck has that got to do with you?'

Maybe he *had* recognised me, I was his dad after all.

'Just asking,' I said. Then, 'How are you, Harry.'

'Passable.'

'Good. That's good.'

Then there was another silence which I filled with pretending to myself that I was about to say the right thing, which I knew was never going to happen, because it had never happened in all the time that Harry had been a part of my life. In the end I gave up pretending to myself and I asked him, 'How about going for a nice cup of tea at Morrison's?'

And he looked at me; straight at me; with that old

familiar angry look, and then he took hold of the string with his thin, bony fingers, and I knew I was about to be in a whole lot of pain, but even with all the years of practice I'd had while Harry was growing up, I wasn't ready for what happened next. Because he pulled that string so hard that it pulled my heart right out of my chest, and all I could do was watch, sitting there trying to breathe, with the dog whining and sniffing and tangling itself around my legs. Then he stood up, and before he walked away, swinging my heart to and fro, on the end of that string, he looked at me like he knew it was the last time, and he said, 'Fuck off, Frank.'

Johannesburg

by Joe Bedford

It was me who insisted we travel by rail. Rhodes tried to
laugh off the idea, since it tripled the length and cost of our
trip, but in the end I simply refused to take a flight, and he
walked off while I was explaining the absurdity of taking
a budget airline to a conference on organic farming. Now,
with the conference behind us, the fact that we're stuck
together on this train for the next thirty-six hours sits heavy
in my stomach. As we pull out of Johannesburg, he unpacks
a few things in silence and slams the cabin door on the way
out. Maybe he'll manage to sulk all the way to Cape Town.
The conference hosted speakers from all over the world. At
first, Rhodes made a point of asking delegates how they'd
got to Johannesburg, and then saying:

'Naturally. Good flight?'

But after a beer he seemed to enjoy mingling with the
farmers. He was lively and candid, and stood out from the
start. Most of the delegates were well-spoken and zealous
about the environment. All of them but me were white.
Rhodes showed no embarrassment explaining that we paid
for New Promise Farm with the money he makes restoring
motorbikes. I had to stop him forcing a group of Americans
to look at pictures of his Harley. I heard him tell someone
the farm would run him into the ground. When he noticed
I'd heard him, he just shrugged.Running New Promise has
been difficult, it's true. It's a sandy tract of land overgrown
with invasive Port Jackson willow which we're still clearing
after three years. We pump water from a borehole and
store it in ferrocement tanks. Our beds produce just enough
vegetables to feed ourselves and our son Dion, and to keep
a small stall at a farmers' market. But without Rhodes's
business we'd have nothing at all.

He won't admit it, but this one inescapable fact underlies every discussion we've ever had about the farm. It surfaces constantly in the form of sighs, grunts, glances. Despite the fact I run the farm by myself, the look in Rhodes's eye when I bring him an unexpected outgoing that he sees me, ultimately, as a frittering housewife. Even if I am the one with the dirt under their nails.The cabin door opens but I ignore it. The sun is high over Gauteng. My stomach turns as he sits down.

'Sorry,' he says. I worry he's going to make his apologies now, before I'm prepared. 'It's Opa.'

His father – an old-fashioned Afrikaner who raised Rhodes on an intensive farm, since lost.

'He wants to know whether the compost can be turned.'

All through the weekend, Rhodes has been texting his parents back and forth as they watch the farm. Their questions have been mostly banal – some so banal that I can sense their scepticism of my methods, as if I were trying to heave up every basic fundament of agriculture. They've directed all their questions to Rhodes, who knows nothing about the farm and so has deferred to me every single time. The only question they texted me directly was where I kept the detergent. I explain about the compost without looking away from the window. I know he's noticed my nervous breathing. Fuck him for putting me in this position. Everything within me wants to get out of the cabin. Then he jumps up, mumbles another apology and leaves.

My heart beats furiously inside my chest. A flash of misery runs through me. Yes. Maybe this is the end. There's nothing to do on this train – I spend the whole day staring out of the window. And now the light is failing and I'm thinking of my parents. They lived happily together right up until my mother's death. My father went soon after, complicit with his illness and eager to follow her. Their relationship was difficult – my father white English, my mother Cape Coloured. My father's father disowned him, and my mother faced prejudice throughout her life. Regardless, they worked hard and moved up quickly. Their relationship with Rhodes'sparents, who they met infrequently in the last years of their life, never really extended beyond formalities. Their accord was quiet and polite and nothing more.

When Rhodes and I married, few people took exception – only Rhodes's most distant cousins questioned my heritage. Dion was born into a happy family. Then we took the farm. We coasted for about a year on the excitement of the purchase, working all hours to clear the land, while I read widely and led the designs. We chatted long into the dark country nights, over bonfires of Port Jackson. But the first summer scorched our beds and split our tank. From then on, the hitches hammered at us from every side. By the time Dion started school, Rhodes and I were sleeping in separate beds. We hadn't slept together since, until four nights ago in a single-bedded cabin identical to this one, on the way to the conference. We'd actually been happy that night, leaving New Promise behind us. The prospect of sharing a bed with him after what happened in Johannesburg horrifies me. But where else is he supposed to sleep tonight?

Rehearsals of the argument we're going to have muddy up my head. It's just too much.The train is long and full – I find Rhodes towards the back. Judging by the men sat on the floor by the carriage door, I guess he's paid someone to take their seat. He's snoring with his mouth open, the only white person in the carriage. The argument I'd rehearsed dissolves into wasted emotion. I consider taking the bottle cradled in the crook of his arm, as I'd done on Friday night when Yusuf – our host in Johannesburg – found him unconscious in the garage.

Christ, I want to shout at him. But I think better of it. Instead, I march back and shut myself in the cabin. Outside, the countryside is black and empty. Somewhere, farmers are bedding down, bushmen are drinking and

laughing. Dion will already be in bed. I force out a few
useless tears, and sleep.I wake with a start. Rhodes is
sitting under the window. The train is stationary, the
engine running. I pull the covers up over my body.

'We're at Kimberley,' he says. 'About 45 minutes.'

I rub my eyes. 'What do you want?'

Normally, a snap like this would provoke an argument.
He seems to consider one.

'Text from Opa.' His voice is flat. 'The pump's lost
pressure.'

I give the instructions bitterly. My phone rings.

'Is it my mother?' he asks while texting.

My throat tightens. 'No.'

I try to put the phone down as if I'm already thinking of
something else but he's looking right at me.

He knows. 'Well?'

I stare out at Kimberley Station, but too much time has
passed. He'll only ask again.

'It was Yusuf.'

I hold his gaze for the first time since Johannesburg.
He's the one to break it.

'So what does he want?'

He wants to apologise for not being there for me on
Sunday.

'I don't know, I didn't answer it.'

Now there'll be a fight. I watch him fetch 50 rand from
his suitcase and then, without a word, walk to the door.
He pauses there and for a moment an old instinct of pity
tries to make me say something but I hold my tongue.
Poor stupid man. The door clicks shut and the train pulls
out of Kimberley. It was never a secret that Rhodes hated
Yusuf. It had nothing to do with the fact that Yusuf and
I fooled around at university, but more to do with some
fundamental rivalry that I will never understand. Yusuf is
disliked by most average South Africans. He wears tie-dye
and sandals and lets his hair grow long and uncombed. His
business card lists 'Freelance Consultant' – his usual work

– underneath 'Free Spirit'.

Typically, his conversation turns quickly to veganism, ley lines, conspiracy theories, his amalgam of religious beliefs. What he rarely mentions is his given name – George – or his divorce or the twin girls she took with her, whom he never gets to see. He was keen to put us up for the conference. When in Johannesburg, he stays in a gated community in Sandton which Rhodes always reminds me was inherited from his grandparents. Though that's always whispered. Rhodes was relieved that the talks kept him tied up for most of the weekend. So it was only in the evenings that tensions were allowed to flare.

Friday night passed smoothly. We'd just arrived and Yusuf threw a party for the delegation. When Rhodes passed out in the garage, Yusuf proclaimed a personal victory against alcohol that my husband was too drunk to remember. But on Saturday, when the three of us sat alone at Yusuf's dining table, I knew instinctively that there would be an argument. Conversation was slow at first, mostly around the conference. When Yusuf diverted it towards extra terrestrial life, Rhodes ate in complete silence until the subject passed. I was bored by the adolescent tension coming from my husband, so I introduced a topic I knew we'd all agree on.

'Springboks are looking good this year.'

Rhodes picked up immediately. Even Yusuf, who'd systematically tried to shed his links with 'George', couldn't resist the schoolyard excitement of rugby. We stayed on course right through dessert, until Rhodes said in passing: 'Should get Dion into the school team.'

The slight lull that followed was noticeably protracted. Rhodes was suspicious – he thought he'd said something innocuous.

Yusuf took the initiative. It was in the wrong direction.

'You know my feelings on the school system. I'm still trying to get the twins out of there.'

Yusuf had homeschooled his daughters until they

were taken away, something we had been talking about extensively over the phone. Maybe I shouldn't have, but I kept these calls from Rhodes, knowing it would be easier to open the debate if I'd made up my own mind first. I didn't realise until then that I already had.

'School is crucial at that age,' said Rhodes. 'It's where you learn about the world.'

'Exactly.' Yusuf became smug. 'Laws, punishments, competition, conformity.'

Rhodes's voice rose as he counted on his fingers. 'Education. Your mates. Sense of responsibility.'

The pair spoke over each other until Rhodes tried to bring me into it.

'We spoke about it briefly before, didn't we?'

'Yes. Briefly.'

Another awkward silence. Rhodes asked if I'd been thinking about it. I told him I had.

'For Dion?'

'Of course for Dion!'

He seemed genuinely surprised. I explained my recent feelings about Dion's school, feelings I'd only so far discussed with Yusuf. I told him I was confident I could school Dion myself while maintaining the farm.

'This is unbelievable,' said Rhodes, and I wasn't surprised.

I thought for a moment he was going to square off to Yusuf, who seemed suddenly desperate to leave the table. Instead it was Rhodes who got up and left. He took a taxi into the city and arrived back at midnight. I assumed by his quietness that he wanted to drop the subject until we got back to New Promise. I conceded.

We slept in the twins' room, laid flat on their separate single beds, surrounded by the drawings and exercises of their homeschooling, marked in red by their father. I'm half-asleep when Rhodes returns to the cabin. It's noon, which means we're only a few hours from Cape Town. The fact that he's slumped into his seat tells me that he plans on staying put for the rest of the journey. Fine. So let him sulk. Awkward silences, though painful, have long since been the norm. So I'm stunned to hear his voice.

'We have to talk about Dion.'

Christ. Is this it then? Is one of us finally going to broach the D-word? Or does he want to have the conversation he tried to start on Sunday, in the final hours of the conference, the conversation we can never go back from? I straighten up.

'You want to talk about homeschooling?' I say. 'Now? You're pathetic.'

The bitterness spurs me on. He takes it painlessly.

'I don't want it discussed in front of him,' he says. Pathetic.

'Well, of course not, Rhodes. Who in their right mind would ask their child what they wanted?'

'That's not what I mean.'

'If you want to talk, go ahead. I'll just sit here.'

'That's unfair.'

'Unfair?' I'm losing control of the situation. 'You're ridiculous.'

The memory of Sunday afternoon is rushing to my head – the hush in the conference room, the eyes of the delegates.

'Look,' he says, 'We can talk about Sunday when we––'

The train is suddenly hot and dizzying. Outside I see the vineyards of the Western Cape glow yellow. Loud, open tears are falling into my hands. Rhodes hugs me automatically and I can't help but let him. I shake in his arms, and the images overwhelm me. In my mind it's Sunday again, and I'm back in Johannesburg.

***

We spoke little over breakfast that morning. Yusuf had left and the dining table was already associated with things unsaid. I knew Rhodes would drink at the conference, but I was surprised to see him bring the quarter-bottle of whiskey he'd brought back from the city the night before. I told him it wouldn't help but he wandered off and started speaking loudly to people in Afrikaans. I mingled, spoke with Yusuf, lost sight of Rhodes. I didn't see him until we broke for lunch.

Everyone convened in the main hall for buffet food. I guessed correctly that he'd skipped the morning's talks, and that he'd already finished the whiskey. But something trivial had put him in a good mood – perhaps he'd met a like-minded Afrikaner. I knew it was only the volatile good humour of a drunk. I tried to relax him but couldn't. He started bothering the Americans who he'd shown his Harley to the morning before. They edged away. Then he made a public display of opening a beer bottle with his teeth, something I hadn't seen him do since before New Promise. I tugged his arm and told him to simmer down. He started singing. When I told him again, he turned.

'I'm an adult.'

'Act like one.' I should've dropped it. 'You're embarrassing me.'

I whispered that I knew he was upset about last night, but that we'd have plenty of time to talk everything over when we got home.

'Nothing to say. You're not taking my son out of school.'

'Our son. Besides, it'll be a joint decision.'

'Exactly. And I'm saying no.'

I tried to draw him away from the centre of the room but he wouldn't budge. People were looking.

'He's not going.'

'Rhodes.'

'No.' He tottered. 'He's not going.'

The beer-bottle fell out of his hand and bounced awkwardly on the carpet. I picked it up and kept it. An empty circle formed around us.

'Rhodes, you're drunk. I'm leaving.'

I was about to go when it happened. It was so sudden

and messy and public.

Rhodes opened his mouth and the words fell out of him greasy and devastating. 'I'm not letting my boy grow up like a barefoot *kaffir*.'

And that was it. The word, carrying with it all the pain and hatred of the past, tumbled clumsily into a weekend full of talk of the future. The delegates around us fell silent as their pity descended upon me. Their hatred and fear of Rhodes settled in the air around us.

'Poor woman,' they must have been thinking, 'The only person of colour at the entire conference and her husband shouts the word "*kaffir*" at her.'

Already the Americans had guessed by the crowd's reaction what it meant. The shame was complete. I looked around for Yusuf. He didn't come forward. I ran out of the conference hall in a blur and met the streets of Johannesburg blinded by tears. I slumped down there, anonymous, and all the passing people of the Black capital saw a sight so commonplace they might barely have noticed. A woman of colour, crying on the pavement.

***

The train is pulling into Cape Town. We sit opposite each other, Rhodes and I, watching the townships take shape. My mother grew up in a place like that, after her family was displaced from the city, before she met my father. They raised me to value the same freedom and contentment they wished for everyone. They would understand little, I think, of the relative discomfort of New Promise Farm, but they might have understood my desire to create a better world for my family. Now we're returning to that better world, but my images of it are cold and overcast. I see the broken pump of the borehole, the cracks in the ferrocement. I see the Port Jackson willow, impossible to clear, choking the native fynbos and our vegetables and livelihood, surrounding the main house, bearing down on us. I have no idea what will happen tonight, when Rhodes's parents have gone, and Dion is in bed. I have no idea what Rhodes and I will say to each other, if anything. I don't know what will happen to the farm or to my family. For this moment, like my mother boarding the bus to take her out of town, the certainty of the absolute present is the only certainty there is. So we alight at Cape Town in the chaos of baggage and the crowd.

Gambles and Balances
by Bruce Harris

She stands by the window on the upstairs landing, which
she concedes to herself is probably her favourite window in
the house. There is always considerable competition. She
has lived here with Peter for over 20 years, loving the house
from the start, with its sweeping Somerset countryside
views to the rear, even if the front view is mostly their
neat estate of 'executive housing'. The landing window
overlooks their side garden and then the fields beyond.
The side garden is mostly lawn, and in the early morning,
blackbirds would scavenge across it, their little feet darting
comically if frantically across the grass. When the children
were children, this had been a strategically useful point for
checking that normal mornings were proceeding in due
order and no bodies had failed to emerge. Peter had always
particularly cherished their en suite bathroom;

'It's wonderful, Jane, to not have to compete with the
kids, much as I love them; they're so unpredictable in
the morning'. The two children, Richard and Kate, could
sometimes seem like a dozen. Now every morning is
peaceful, and she sometimes finds herself thinking that
there can be too much peace. She realizes that, favourite
view as it is, she seeks the distraction of it when her mind is
troubled.

Now it isn't morning, it's Friday evening, with Peter on
the weary trek back from another interminable London
conference, where he'd been for four days. His optimistic
time of arrival was in 20 minutes; he would normally have
phoned from half an hour away, so a customary seed of
anxiety within her has already found its fertile soil. In the
distance, she can see his turn-off from the M5. She thinks
she might catch a glimpse of his big blue car, triggering

the Friday homecoming sequence of beginning the food, choosing a wine and checking the hot water for his soak-off-London bath. Familiar routines to bridge the work and weekend gap, before the boat and golf clubs for occasional visits, yes, with Peter's persona adjusting slightly from his tongue-in-cheek golf club neo-conservatism, mostly to tease some far-right members, to the more scurrilous wit of the boat club, too laddish for Jane's taste. Now and then, there would be home or away entertaining; even more occasionally, in recent months, visits from the 'children', one now with children of his own. But mostly reading, garden pottering, picking the better television.

Her face freezes momentarily as she remembers his usual Friday returning demeanour; moody, monosyllabic, sometimes rather rumpled, his blue suit dishevelled after he'd driven in it. She suddenly sees clearly enough that her assumption that he is simply shaking off the road travel is just that – an assumption.

Peter's nature is to be where the action is, to compete, to exercise authority; does he actually find weekends tedious? Is he now sitting disconsolately in some service station bracing himself to leave the real world for what he sees as a domesticated, premature old age? She is disturbed enough by the thought to retreat to the bedroom, sitting on the bed beside the phone willing it to ring and replace malicious speculation with routine practicalities. By the time he has bathed and had a glass of wine, he is more amiable – even, on occasion, amorous, although not much recently. Usually, when she takes a glass to him, he is already in the bath, and she enjoys the intimacy of talking to him on a stool next to it. And yes, she thinks, the intimacy includes his nudity; he has never 'let himself go' and she is still comfortable with his body. He is still good-looking, even with less hair than there used to be and eyes more frequently misted over with tiredness. If his libido was no longer as emphatic, it was a natural progression.

But, once again, a thought strikes like a blow. A middle-

aged man, returning to domesticity flushed and dishevelled
– from what, exactly? These never-ending conferences
- what do they actually amount to? Why so necessary, for
a well-established professional man in his early 50s? Yes,
he'd showed her the programme for this one – human
resources, personnel optimising, standard management
gobbledegook, but why so many "How to Manage"
conferences rather than just managing? Yes, he'd phoned
her from the hotel, but on his mobile - technically speaking,
he could be anywhere.

She sighs and kicks her shoes off to put her feet up
on the bed. So, so silly. The bed retains the scent of him,
even after four days; his soap, his aftershave, that fresh
air thing he carries with him because he spends so much
time outdoors, golf, boats, walking. They had been married
for nearly 30 years; she knew every facet of him, every
face, every mood, she had borne his children. It verged on
paranoia to imagine he would go to the lengths of inventing
conferences to cover his affairs. And her domesticity was
his preference; even after the children had grown up, he
was still not entirely happy with her part-time helping out
in play school. When she'd said the boisterousness of the
toddlers was beginning to exhaust her, he'd been absolutely
sympathetic and understanding.

'You've done your bit, Jane, with our kids and other
people's. One of us needs to put our feet up, and if it's you,
I'm happy with that – it won't be too long before I join you!'

She stands up and goes to the bedroom window
overlooking the estate. It is September, and Paul Knowles,
the boy next door, a University student and runner, does
his training runs every morning during the summer so as to
be fit for the new term.

'If it's three months of just working in a shop, Mrs.
Tyler, I'll be right out of condition, and the coach will have
something to say about that!'

Paul Knowles is 20 – nearly 21. They'd known him
all his life, baby, toddler, amiable child, sullen teenager,

presentable young man, and he calls them Mr and Mrs Tyler as he always has. On a sultry autumn evening like this, he wears minimal kit, a bare-shouldered vest and tiny shorts. She discreetly watches him coming up the drive from a reflected angle in the wardrobe mirror, with a little mental slap on her naughty wrist. Who would have thought gawky little Paul, all limbs and teeth, would turn into such a gorgeous specimen? She sees no reason why a sophisticated middle-aged woman shouldn't take pleasure in an attractive young man, and Paul's departure from boyhood was now very obvious.

Again, a bolt of a thought roots her to the spot, gazing from young runner to bed and back. If she, in her housebound domesticity, could still find some handsome youth to peep at, where does Peter do his peeping, and who at, and is it just peeping, out in the wide world where closer activity than peeping is easy and recipients plentiful? She is a mature woman who can see such indulgences as harmless fun, even when occasional daydreams pop into her mind involving Paul. Peter is a mature, experienced man, with opportunities available – conferences, hotels, PAs, secretaries, girl employees 'wanting to get on' – what are his fantasies and peeping points, and is a man so assertive going to be as content as she is for daydreams to remain daydreams?

She hovers as Paul clatters back into the Knowles front garden; the near nakedness of him at close quarters momentarily startles and intrigues her. She moves towards the phone. This is unfair of Peter; there will need to be some explanation. She was afraid that he might even now be entangled in a motorway pile-up, his phone crushed under a lorry's wheels, possibly exactly as she is admiring the boy next door. She leaves the bedroom, to move away from marriage headquarters and give herself space to think, and goes into the family bathroom.

Once the children's and now effectively no one's for most of the time, its neglect reflected in pressed towels and

presentation cosmetics, mostly unopened, except for Peter's
wet shaving things. He comes in here for a 'proper shave',
supposedly because the mirror is bigger and the light better
than the en suite. He leaves the door slightly open, and she
speaks to him en passant as he shaves, inconsequential
pleasantries answered in similar spirit. And what happens
afterwards, she wonders? An impatient, raised eyes look
in the mirror? A sotto voce mutter? Does he actually go
in there to escape her ubiquitous being around him, and
resent her invasions of his privacy?

Still, infuriatingly, no phone. By now, he should be
here, the clunk-whirr of the garage door announcing his
return, so that by the time the door shuts, they will be
in their weekend together, their uninterrupted idyll, or
perhaps a one-sided idyll. She stomps down to the kitchen,
determined to start on the food and resolved to remain
cool. After five minutes peeling and chopping carrots, the
phone rings in the hall and she rushes thankfully towards
it, thinking traffic jams, weather, conference delays in
winding up. It takes 10 seconds for her to register the
moronic deadness of the silence, yet another ridiculous
call centre. Big, sudden and shaming tears, a whole mist of
them, and she rushes upstairs to the en suite bathroom, the
inner sanctum, accessible only to herself and her husband.

She faces herself in the mirror; a strange figure, she
pronounces scornfully within, to burst into tears and
run around the house like some demented teenager.
Smooth, well-preserved skin, the wrinkles minimized and
the face still with dignity and some beauty, though the
thin cheekbones seem even more so and there are two
inescapable age lines just below the dark green eyes. The
hair still with its shape, even if a little too WI guest speaker
correct, and undeniably with streaks of grey which she,
like Peter, refuses to dye out. The most unsightly features,
beyond any doubt, are the two tear streaks, and she washes
them away with a gesture of impatience.

Whatever has delayed Peter will be explained in its

entirely logical ramifications, most probably within the next half-hour. Perhaps, she thinks, stopping work altogether wasn't such a good idea. Much as she loves Peter, she doesn't really want to spend her whole life in his waiting room. If small children were too exhausting, receptionist somewhere, perhaps the health centre, meeting people and doing something useful. Maybe even a desk at the local leisure centre, with its Olympic standard pool, where if she really wanted to, she could gorge herself on near-naked young men until she became more connoisseur than dabbler. She grins wickedly at herself and marvels at the way the under-eye lines suddenly gravitate to the sides and give her a quite sinister, predatory look. At the same moment, one eye tugs to the left and the little shelf where Peter keeps his collection of aftershaves. Travel usually meant topping up and usually he had five or six there. She had teased him about it: 'How many fragrances do you need, darling?', to be answered with his quiet smile. Now there were only two, meaning he had gone to some week-long dull management-fest equipped with at least three aftershaves.

The mirror again, and this time the image is of a credulous fool, an old mare put out to grass while the still-virile husband plays about in various temps' and assistants' beds and lives.

She stamps downstairs and sits heavily down in the hall, on the phone seat, and calls to mind his mobile number. Now she is strongly inclined to call, whether he's in the car or not; voicemail could at least tell him in no uncertain terms that twiddling her thumbs in painful ignorance was not how she would be treated, not now or in whatever future might be left. She saw someone, perhaps that unsubtle creature Yvonne, who Peter's colleague Douglas Caldwell laughably described as a personal assistant, next to him in the car.

'Number flashing, Peter; don't recognize it. Out in the

sticks, by the look of it'.

Peter stops at a traffic light and glances over.

'God, darling, that's the wife. Oh, hell's bells...' – glances at watch – '...yes, she would've started cooking and clucking by now, all set for a cosy old night and sod horrid old London for another week – '

No, no, no. She closes her eyes. Peter is not like that. He does respect her, and any woman can tell when a man genuinely cares for her; his solicitude around her, the gentleness of his voice, the kindnesses and favours he does her. Peter knew how to treat her. Peter knew how to treat women. And with opportunity and appetite, which no doubt he still had, even if it wasn't necessarily for what she had to offer...

She opens her eyes and looks, suddenly critically, at the objects in the hall, the wall clock, the occasional table, the landscape painting, the old-fashioned solid wooden hatstand, the whole a declaration of taste to whoever arrived at the house.

And every last object chosen by her. Where were they when she selected that wall clock, such a contemporary feel to it – had he been with her at the time? The hatstand she did remember, a high street antique furniture shop, and she finds herself admiring it for a well- constructed, solid, reassuring old object – 'Peter!' she shouts delightedly to somewhere behind her, 'This will finally do away with that dreadful coat rack threatening to fall off the wall'. Non-committal grunt to her right. 'Do try to take an interest, darling'. 'What? – yes, of course, whatever you think best. You're the decor expert, darling'.

Now she inspects the hall in detail, recording everything, the carpet, the carefully watered real flowers on the occasional table, everything chosen and maintained by her. And, for that matter, the same applies to every other room; her choices, to which he graciously assents, probably because of a line of least resistance, bar occasional, mild semi-protests – 'Bit over the top on the fluffy cushions, aren't we, darling?' 'Do we need so much foliage, when Richard still has that persistent hay fever?' – but peripheral protests that do not threaten anything drastic. If you don't care, you don't argue. 'If it's what she wants, what the hell? I'm a quiet life man'. She could hear him saying it, especially in the boat club – 'I'm a quiet life man'.

These rooms are like the chambers of my mind, she thinks, the compartments of my being – cleanliness room, love room, food and entertaining room, room where I look out to think about the world outside on the condition that it never gets inside, all to my design and taste and all inhabited almost entirely by me. People come to take a trip around my mind, my tastes, my creative abilities, and return to the world to get on with their lives. I have made myself a beautifully accessorized prison while my husband prowls happily and satisfyingly around the real world, coming to see me for visiting time.

Now she suddenly finds herself in the utility room between the kitchen and the garage. She has a pill drawer there, something only she knows about, perhaps because no one else is interested. In the drawer is a miscellaneous accumulation of medicines, some for ailments now forgotten about, some of them for others still irritatingly persistent, all of them hers. She stands and stares, knowing full well moving beyond looking at them will mean feeling, selecting and judging. That Rubicon is yet to be crossed.

Something in her is hoping it will never be, another is breathing insidiously that there is a case good enough to be at least considered. No old age, no possibility whatever of being abandoned, humiliated in front of children and grandchildren, left with no life by a man after giving so much of hers to his, left to wonder desolately through the rooms of her mind peeping out at a world she dare not re-join. All in a few minutes, a simple, conclusive act, ending all speculation, all fear, all striving to understand, even after so long, who or what she is married to. If she must be forever adrift in her badly steered boat, perhaps the time might have arrived to just mercifully sink it. She stands and looks, she weighs the gambles and balances, and the angels and demons fight inside her for the right to hold sway over the life she has left.

Light and noise from the garage; the clunking and whirring begins. She closes her eyes again, already seeing him at ease in the bath, his eyes mellowing, dissecting for her the nonsense language of management seminars, the absurd vanities of his grander colleagues. She opens her eyes, bangs the drawer shut and hurries into the kitchen to hack at the carrots again, 10 seconds before he clatters in behind her.

'Jane, darling, I am so, so sorry'. His scent is behind her, the fresh air, the aftershave selection. 'I simply could not get a signal; I kept trying, in lay-bys, services, everywhere. Even a couple of efforts at a payphone, occupied by someone apparently telling their life story into it. And the traffic so heavy that every delay just made matters worse. I'm going to get on to the company who sold me the thing and play hell... twenty-first-century technology...God...'

She takes a long time to drop off to sleep, two eyes wide in the dark, turned away from his steady, even breathing on her right. She has resolved to clear the pill drawer, disposing of everything past its sell-by, probably meaning everything. Somewhere inside her a silent scream remains unextinguished, and an oddly persistent question mark still sits insolubly over the aftershave shelf.

VITA

Vita

by Rachael Hill

A flash of scarlet amongst the brown, cream, and grey catches my eye, aching to be seen. I turn to look and see the owner of the scarlet standing across the room. She is a *she*. She isn't looking at me. It's a small gallery; she is perhaps only ten feet away. The scarlet is her hair, cut in a stylish bob that curves and ends just above dainty, angular shoulders clad in a dark brown coat reaching almost to her knees, and tied at the waist. I'm looking at her side on and can see her cardinal hair is cut in a sharp fringe that ends just as it reaches her eyebrows. I think that to own such hair she must have green eyes, and they would be piercing, like a fox.

We're in an art gallery, and she is a piece of art herself. The paintings littering the walls no longer hold my interest: paling in comparison to the living, breathing work I see before me. When she leaves, she'll take the gallery's greatest piece. She's standing to my left; I can see her right side in perfect profile, as if she's been sliced in half and presented this way. I can tell she's slight, though the long, brown coat gives little away. Slender legs wrapped in black leggings extend from beneath the coats hem, completed with solid black boots sporting forest green laces; the same shade I imagine her eyes to be. A mustard scarf erupts from between the lapels of the coat, clutching at her pale throat. Pearly skin coats sharp cheekbones, a small nose, and a delicately pointed chin, yielding to thin dark lips and eyes I cannot see. Her hands are in her pockets and a dark brown leather messenger bag slung across her left shoulder, resting on her right hip.

I'm transfixed; I don't think I've ever seen something

so beautiful. I wonder if I ever will again. For a second, I dare to imagine. She senses me watching, turns, catches my eye and holds my gaze. That moment is the longest of my life. In it, she holds me gently with those eyes as green as I knew they would be. Through them she whispers to me softly, invites me to go with her, join her, know her. I'm filled with longing to do just that. In this moment that lasts a lifetime, anything is possible, and I know I'm standing at the precipice of a choice that will shape everything. In a few short steps I could close the space between us, accept her invitation, and begin the future. Her gaze requests it.

Yet I do not. I blink and look away, breaking contact, feeling the colour rise to my cheeks, vibrant, matching her hair. In a heartbeat I realize my mistake. I look back, but she has already turned away. The moment is lost to the past. It takes less than a second for the surge of self-hatred to rise like bile in the back of my throat. It's too late; I must live with myself.

That night I dream of dancing with a scarlet woman cast in moonlight. When I wake, she's a dream fading quickly with the fog of night, lost to the chasm of my subconscious mind. I dress, make breakfast, spend time drawing. Try to draw something, anything, other than the red-haired woman. I fail. Then, I catch the bus to the city centre, where I meet my partner, Ruby, for a late lunch. In contrast to her name, Ruby is a washed-out palette of plain tones: brown, white, grey, and pink. There is nothing remarkable to catch the eye. Our relationship is much the same. We eat sandwiches, drink coffee and talk about the banal things we've done since we last met. I tell her about the museum, but not about the woman with the scarlet hair.

Some months later, I start a new job with a higher wage, allowing me to begin thinking about the future. My mother fusses: says it's high time I started taking that future seriously. I'm in my late 20s; I should be thinking about houses and children, a wife. The path is laid before me. So, I ask Ruby to marry me. She accepts, of course, and we have a small wedding in the local church. I never wanted a church wedding, but Ruby's parents are staunch Christians. The church was a compromise; in return, I get the final say on the house we decide to buy almost six months later.

The mid-terrace red brick house feels unloved, but the estate agent, who smells heavily of sickly rose fragrance and reminds me uncannily of an actress I cannot name, assures us it has potential. We consolidate our funds and buy it. It's not far from our previous homes, and the city is still only a short bus journey away. Moving in is punctuated with almost arguments, meddlesome family members, champagne bubbles, and the worst hangover since the wedding. Perhaps it says something about these happy life events; that you drink so much you remember barely anything, and wake suffering the next day. I take on extra work to afford the higher mortgage repayments Ruby thinks are a good idea. This house is our first step on the ladder, not our forever-home.

Over the following year, we make some effort to turn the unloved red brick house into a home, but the building is stubborn, and we are met with disgruntled draughts and rebellious damp. We talk about moving but Ruby is adamant that, if we make just a few more improvements, it'll sell for more and we can afford better next time. With screams and wails, baby-sick, and the smell of shit, children permeate our lives. First one, then two, then a third. By then we don't have to worry about making any more because there's no time for sex. I take on extra work so that Ruby can stay home with the children. I don't draw anymore. I'm now a husband, a Dad and a mortgage owner: an overworked middle-aged man who comes home to a wife too tired to make love.

We don't talk anymore. Like housemates, we cohabit the same space, tied together by the three small lives we brought into the world. Ruby is tired, she looks ill, she puts on weight and starts buying gossip magazines. She develops a posse of mothers who surround her, a cackling shroud of exaggerated femininity. I keep my distance.

Our children grow from screaming sprogs to bouncing frogs. They're happy. I'm a good father; I go to school shows, football matches, dance performances. My daughter is the middle child and when teenage comes, it hits her hardest. One day she flounces home from a friend's house with bright claret hair, and I'm reminded briefly of a woman I once saw in a museum. But the image lasts only a moment, and although I said barely anything my daughter is screaming and marching to her bedroom, slamming her door. I don't know what to do, so I leave her to it.

Ruby loses the weight she'd gained, releases her cackling shroud, starts smoking cigarettes, and I find empty vodka bottles reflecting the green of the recycling bin. There are heavy bags under her eyes. We try to talk, but there's nothing left to say. I get a small pay rise that is swallowed immediately by a family of five and the demands of a cranky old red brick terrace we never manage to leave. I think that perhaps when my children move out, I'll quit the job that makes me hate myself and go back to my drawing, my art. Maybe then I'll discover the brilliant person behind the alcohol infused partner who sits across the dinner table from me each night.

The chicks fly the nest, until only one is left. The space between Ruby and I is thrown into stark relief, although a void stretches between us, gnawing at our insides, seeping our colours and turning us into monochrome shadows of the people we dreamed we'd be. Then one night she folds; drunken, slurring, she declares enough is enough. She's carried this family alone so far, needs someone who'll be active in her relationship, in her life. By morning, she's gone, and I am left with the remnants of a broken home. Questions oscillate: *What next?* Was this all life had to offer? It's not what I dreamed, long ago. Have I wasted it? Let myself mould to everyone else's ideas, always waiting for someone else to take charge—should it have been me? Always a settler because settling is safer than facing the unknown; standing at the edge never daring to jump. Watching, out the way, letting them get on with it— did I do it all wrong?

The surge of self-hatred rises like bile in the back of my throat. I'm transfixed; I don't think I've ever seen something so beautiful. I wonder if I ever will again. For a moment, I dare to imagine.

She senses me watching, turns, catches my eye and holds my gaze. That moment is the longest of my life. In it she holds me gently with those eyes as green as I knew they would be. Through them she whispers to me softly, invites me to go with her, join her, know her. I'm filled with longing to do just that. In this moment that lasts a lifetime, anything is possible, and I know I'm standing at the precipice of a choice that will shape everything. In a few short steps I could close the space between us, accept her invitation, and begin the future. Her gaze requests it.

I cross the room and she smiles at me, dark lips revealing straight white teeth. I ask her name: Elise. Together, we explore the gallery, laughter rising in champagne bubbles from our dancing lips. We go for dinner, and her forest green eyes whisper to me over my forgotten fish and wine while our words mingle excitedly. She is a thinker and has much to say. We talk about art, and our dreams; we talk about the world, love, desire. Later, we are burning passion amongst the crumpled sheets; electric skin soliciting orgasms that shake our understanding of human, of together. We lie, panting and heavy, in each other's arms.

I break up with Ruby; letting her down gently, I inadvertently save us from a life we only think we want. I never see her again. My mother is angry, disappointed; says it's high time I took the future seriously: I'm in my late twenties—I should be thinking about houses and children, a wife. I'm a fool not to walk the path laid before me. Elise and I travel; long weeks spent tasting the corners of the world. We laugh, dance, sing, love, and cry together. She urges me to quit the job that sucks the breath from my lungs. I'm scared, but she feeds my soul; reminds me I'm an artist, that life is for passion and colour. She writes and sings, I draw and paint. Combined, we make enough to keep our small world afloat. I paint her in all the colours of the rainbow, but even then, they're not enough to do her credit. She is a living technicolour dream.

We marry on white sands beneath a laughing sun, to the waves' crashing applause. There, our families meet for the first time, and celebrate. When our children come, we're ready, and they grow steady and strong. Their playgrounds are the untamed beach and the dappled depths of the forest. They have their mothers red hair and their father's eye for beauty. I'm a husband and a daddy. I'm a person, a lover, a friend, an artist. I'm a stroke of vibrant colour upon my life's canvas.

Our children grow fast: two girls and a boy. They're creatures of the world, wild and untameable. I teach them, and guide them, to think beyond the barriers of their minds. In return, their dreams expand beyond the spaces they've grown from, stretching across seas and mountains. They are clever, courageous, grounded, ambitious. One by one they take their leave, and though their paths may be difficult, I know they'll be ok: they are made of the stuff of dreams. Then they're gone, and they leave behind a space, a hole: the hush that falls when the storm has passed. But the two people either side of it are partners, and they close the gap: begin a new story.

Missing the Boat
by Vivian Oldaker

Ted sat on the scrubby grass, watching the water slap against the peeling hull of the rowing boat. The rope mooring it to the jetty was old and frayed; it belonged to the people in the house opposite. They would soon have to replace the rope or risk losing the boat, which had certainly seen better days. It had a name, but Ted couldn't bring the blur of letters into focus. He took his binoculars from the front pocket of his rucksack and the words '*Summer Promise*' swam into view. The sun was burning the top of his head; he had neglected to bring his old straw trilby to the river. It was August, the heat relentless and the string of sunny days seemingly endless. Three rambunctious teenage boys occupied the nearby bench. It bore an inscription:

In Memory of Daphne Roberts Who Loved This Place 1934 – 2018. In fact Daphne, Ted's wife, hadn't particularly loved this place; she'd preferred the spot down by the weir but as that was already blessed with two benches, he'd gone against her wishes. He had seldom done so while she lived. Today was one of those days when Ted felt bleary and bleak. A rook in a nearby alder tree gazed down at him beadily.

The sun ducked behind a cloud and a feeble breeze stirred the still air. Across the water, a hissing, spitting, sprinkler assaulted the lawn of the sprawling bungalow. It hadn't rained for weeks but such wastefulness offended Ted. A fat young man came out of the house wearing a black baseball cap, black jeans and black t-shirt. An odd choice of attire for such a hot day. Perhaps, thought Ted, he was one of those goths, like the grandson of his friend and neighbour John. The youth waddled around the sprinkler to inspect the boat, looked across at Ted, and then retreated indoors.

Ted remembered the dryness of Kenya, where he and Daphne had lived for a decade in an almost colonial style when he worked for Shell. It was in Mombasa that Daphne had lost the baby after a particularly rowdy Saturday night dinner dance. She'd been about five months pregnant. They didn't have scans in those days, certainly not in East Africa; the gestational calculation down to arithmetic and guesswork. The doctor, a kindly man named O'Connor, said it was 'just one of those things.' Funny, thought Ted, that he could remember the doctor's name from all those years ago but struggled to recall the name of John's grandson, a decent young chap despite his wonky black eyeliner and pierced lip. If the baby had lived she might have been a grandmother by now. Ted had wanted to name the child Rose, after his mother, but Daphne - whose philosophy was always 'least said soonest mended' - was unconvinced that the tiny, half-formed being warranted a name at all and had adamantly refused to countenance any kind of ceremony or funeral to mark her death.

There had been no more pregnancies. Daphne had never wanted children in the first place and Ted was frankly terrified at the prospect of fatherhood. While love would not have been deficient, he doubted his ability to raise a child to cope with the world. He had never found it easy himself. A tickle of ants ran over the mountain range of his hand; steadfast, resolute, determined. They were after the remains of someone's ice cream, a pink splat on the grass, a feast fallen from the sky. Ted took his flask from his backpack along with a biography of Cole Porter. He read a few pages, but it was hard to concentrate. He took a swig of water from his flask, wishing he'd brought beer instead. Still, he could no longer drink as he once had and he wanted neither the danger nor the indignity of a wobbly walk home along the riverbank. At his age, the threat of a broken hip was real. It had ambushed John, who had tripped over his cat. Pneumonia. They used to call it 'The old man's friend,' but John had done his best to fight off its advances. When Ted visited him in hospital, John's constant refrain was to blame the cat while simultaneously asking Ted to 'Take care of Tilly if I don't make it.' He hadn't made it. Ted was, however, prevented from assuming continued responsibility for John's feline assassin by John's son, whose daughter - the gothic grandson's younger sister - had demanded its possession.

Ted had been somewhat relieved. He had always preferred dogs, though he hadn't lived with one since Daphne had died. Potter had been a tiny mixed-breed, described by Daphne as a Chimeranian - quite possibly worth his weight in gold, having cost a small fortune to buy. Potter had only outlasted his owner by a month; perhaps sensing that Ted, while dutiful in his care, was never likely to display the abject devotion that both Potter and Daphne had considered his due. Daphne had named the animal after an old friend from the Kenya days. Ted had been perplexed by the choice. Potter the man had been large and hearty; the acknowledged leader of the hard-drinking, hedonistic crew. Potter the dog was small and shivery. Daphne was not known for an ironic sense of humour. When he asked about it she said:

'I was fond of Potter – and little Potter has the same eyebrows.'

Man Potter and Daphne had spent many hours together, swimming in the ocean. Potter with his flabby, hair-speckled back rising from the water like a pale walrus; Daphne with her efficient crawl. It was possible that Potter and Daphne had shared more than an enthusiasm for swimming, but if his wife had fallen for Potter's sweaty charms, she had at least been discreet. Potter had returned to England six months before them and there had been no further contact, save for Christmas 1968, when he had sent a card enclosing a photo of himself standing next to a small motorboat.

On the back he had written: 'Here's me with my latest squeeze: SWELL PARTY. Isn't she gorgeous? Moored near Lymington. Would be super to see you aboard some time.' Daphne had propped the photo on the mantelpiece. She had taken it down several times, gazing at it, chuckling at the choice of name well into the New Year. On Twelfth Night Ted had said:

'You can go see Potter, if you like.'

But Daphne had told him not to be so ridiculous. She had become a stickler for respectability once they had settled in Surrey; constantly concerned with what the neighbours might think, forever keen to keep her head below the parapet of decorum. Their semi-detached home was a symphony in beige; any other choice in interior design considered by Daphne to be 'showy.' After her death, Ted had purchased a pair of blue cushions for the sofa and a framed photographic print of Portofino to place above the mantelpiece. These items went a little way to liven up the monotone in their sterile sitting room.

When sorting through Daphne's things after her death, he had found the photograph of Potter, faded and somewhat creased, in her underwear drawer. Ted did not know whether its location was in any way significant. He had not seen it since that long-ago Christmas. 'Hallo, Potter,' he'd said, looking at it. 'Hallo, Potter, you old bastard. Still alive? I doubt it, matey.'

Vapour trails crossed the sky, blurring into the remaining patch of blue. 'Enough to make a sailor a pair of trousers,' his mother would have said. Ted needed to pee but still he could not stir himself to go home. He felt as though he was waiting, but for what he had no idea. A vintage Riva slid past, bringing in its wake a memory of an Italian holiday, 40 years ago. Ted and Daphne, James and his wife Dolly, who was also Daphne's sister.

The villa had been large and draughty and splendid. One night he and James had jumped on the scooter provided and swerved down the hill to an open-air bar where a covers band was playing. As the musicians launched into Dire Straits's 'Water of Love,' Ted and James had kissed in the shadows. Riding back up the dark hill, Ted had wrapped his arms around James and rested his head on his warm back. They had come to a fork in the road. James had switched off the engine.

'Which way is it back to the villa?'

'It's left,' Ted said. 'Definitely left.'

They went right, returning at last to the villa as the dawn light began to paint the hills. Daphne and Dolly slept on until the sun fully blazed its presence. It seemed neither sister had noticed the overnight absence of a husband. They were all dead now, Daphne, James and Dolly. Ted was the last man standing. He and James had shared just one more kiss on the final night of the holiday. 'Blame it on the moonlight.' James had said.

After that, Ted had done his best to avoid him, facilitated by the epic quarrel between the sisters about – what? He couldn't remember. Thinking of James now, a sadness he'd kept buried for many years rose into his throat. He'd locked his feelings away. Nothing could ever come of them; it was best not to dwell on what might have been, had they both been younger and braver. Or if he had – there was no telling how James might have responded given any further encouragement. Daphne was a demon for holding grudges and they had not attended the funerals of his in-laws. James had pre-deceased Dolly and, a few months after his death, a small package had arrived for Ted. Inside was a note written in Dolly's shaky hand:

'Dear Ted, James wanted you to have this. Sorry you did not come to the funeral. Hope you are both well.' It was a small-scale model of a red Vespa.

'What a ridiculous thing to send!' Daphne had said. 'Put it in the charity bag.'

He had not put it in the charity bag. It was in his pocket right now and his fingers closed over it as they had so often in the years since. From somewhere upstream music was playing. 'Don't stop thinking about tomorrow – don't stop, it'll soon be here.' His shoulders began to ache as iron-grey clouds shuffled in from the west. Was the long drought about to end?

Not long after James' death Ted and Daphne had been drinking tea on their small concrete patio when Daphne had looked up from her magazine and said, apropos of nothing:

'Do you think James was a poofter?'

'What makes you say that?' Ted put his mug down carefully.

'It's in this article –" How to Tell if Your Partner's Gay". I remember the way he used to look at you sometimes, like he wanted to eat you up. Barking up the wrong tree. And he had some very flamboyant shirts; they weren't even fashionable then.'

'Can't say I noticed,' Ted lied. 'Any more of these biscuits?'

'Dolly never hinted,' Daphne said. 'But then, that's Dolly; daft as a brush. Most women would know, but I suppose if James was in the cupboard she might have been blissfully unaware.'

'In the closet.'

'What?'

'The expression is "in the closet", not in the cupboard.'

'Tomayto tomahto. Anyway, closet's American. You know I don't like Americanisms.'

The death of James might have marked a rapprochement between the sisters but it did not. Ted and Daphne had only learned of Dolly's death three years later through her solicitor; she had left everything - a not inconsiderable sum - to a donkey sanctuary in Devon, but had earmarked a photo of their parents in a silver frame for Daphne. 'Typical!' Daphne had said. She had not put the photo on display. Possibly the frame was too ornate for her taste. Ted had pins and needles in his left leg. A pleasure boat chugged past. Several passengers stood on deck including, Ted was surprised to see, his late wife. Daphne beckoned, using her whole arm in the impatient way she'd had when he hadn't complied with sufficient alacrity. Ted looked away at the weeping willow and when he looked back the boat had disappeared under the ironwork bridge. A woman approached with a terrier. The dog licked his hand.

'Are you all right?' she asked.

'Fine and dandy,' Ted said, though he wasn't.

He stroked the dog's feathery ears. 'Just watching the world go by.'

'You should sit on the bench, the grass is getting damp,' she said reprovingly.

The boys had gone. How much time had passed?

'Perhaps I will,' Ted said, 'In a minute.'

He walked stiffly to the bench, sat. The woman strolled on, looking back doubtfully. Ted rubbed his thumb over the lettering on the brass plate.

'What a fool I was, Daphne,' he said out loud.

The sun dimmed again and now the wind had a sharper edge to it. A self-satisfied swan in full sail turned its head to look at Ted, making him smile, despite his discomfort. The old rowing boat across the water finally broke free and began to drift downstream followed by another pleasure boat, moving more slowly than the one bearing Daphne. A single passenger stood on deck. Ted leaned forward to get a better view. James - dear departed, deeply beloved, never forgotten - was leaning against the rail. He blew Ted a kiss, then beckoned gently with one finger. The teenage boys found Ted at the water's edge when they returned a while later equipped with cider cans.

'My first dead body,' one of them said. 'Poor old fucker.'

'At least he's smiling,' his friend took several photos on his phone, lobbed an empty can into the choppy water then called the emergency services, already anticipating the reaction to the story of their evening as it splashed and rippled out through cyberspace.

Here's to You, Mrs. Avery

by Alice Fowler

She sat down on the bed, trying to remember. Something
about the day ahead was different. Something that niggled
in her mind, the way the metal fastening of her skirt jagged
into her back. She tugged her cardigan lower on her hips.
For years it had been her favourite, the wonderful soft
cashmere bought on a trip with Jack to... Ullapool, it must
have been. Silver buttons. An exquisite deep green, the
colour of pine needles. And Jack had let her have it, despite
the price, for cashmere had been special then, something to
drive the length of the country for, to feel against her cheek.
Ruined now, of course.

Not from wear, for Scottish cashmere did last forever,
just as she had promised Jack, in the little shop beside
the loch. Who would have thought then, that that lovely
cardigan would end up stiff and matted, boil washed, no
good to anyone, with her own name, "Avery" scrawled in
ink upon the label? Breakfast: had she had it? Hard to
remember in this unfathomable place. Breakfast: the best
meal of the day, Jack used to say. Though for years she had
contented herself with just an apple.

Had she or hadn't she? She checked her front for
crumbs. No sign of a tray, though sometimes they were
collected without her knowing. She was not hungry, but
that meant nothing. Why did no one tell you when you
were young, to relish the urge to eat? And hungry she had
been – ravenous – rushing in from the cold and cramming
warm bread into her mouth, scrumping fruit, maddened
by her need for food. And now? Never. She could sit all day

in her small square room, eating nothing, and not notice. She swiped one curtain sideways, then the other. What was it about today that made it special? The garden lay below her – how lucky she had been, they had told her, to get this view. She could see the branches of the taller shrubs, the *philadelphus* and *amelanchier*, knitting together against the whiteness of the sky; names she somehow still remembered while other, more useful ones, were gone.

She picked up her looking glass and held it to her face. An instinctive movement, for she had been – and could say it, now she was no longer – a beautiful woman. Not many girls – and again, she could say it now – had been as lucky as she, with her raven curls and Cupid's bow. She had looked like a film star, and had longed to be one; holding up this very mirror, posturing, believing she had a chance. And now – well, she was in her eighties. 83, not counting the four or five stray years she had knocked off long ago. An old lady, whichever way you looked at it. That was what Julie, who did breakfasts, and Nisha, who did teas, saw when they blustered in to see her. Patricia Avery: nice enough, forgetful, won't be with us long. Not the Patricia Avery she had been and still remained inside: a woman who could break a hundred hearts, just by walking down a street.

'But I am that person,' she longed to say, to Julie and the rest. 'I'm here! I haven't changed!'

Through habit, for there was nothing there to please her now, she looked into the glass. A movement, an outline of a form; not herself. But Jack. Jack! What was he doing there? He was standing sideways to her, white hair blown across his pate.

'Jack!' The name burst from her. He was speaking to someone she could not see. She moved the mirror, trying to peer behind him. A glimpse of blue – water – and yes, that little shop with the sun shining on it and the metal roof, corrugated, so thickly grown with moss it was a landscape in itself. Ullapool. There was the woman, smiling across the counter – so graceful those Scots, so long as you did not cross them. And she herself, in that belted dress that vanished long ago, holding the cardigan in her arms as though it were a precious animal.

And Jack was not happy, that was evident by the sagging of his shoulders. Not happy, for the cardigan was expensive; more than they could afford. The woman was gazing at him. And she, Pat, gazing at him too, wanting that cardigan more than anything. And Jack, knowing this, for she could see him wilting further beneath the combined yearning of herself and the woman, who even now was preparing to wrap the feather-light wool in saffron tissue, that only emphasized the perfection of the green.

'Patricia? Penny for them, dear?'

She put the mirror down. Julie's presence filled the room. A clank as the breakfast tray landed on the bedside table.

'Cup of tea, dear?'

She twisted towards the voice. Julie: pink, cheerful, bringer of breakfasts, harbinger of another day. Only – who was this? Mouth hidden; masked like an intruder, or a dog that had been muzzled. Not pink, friendly Julie. A different, alarming Julie, who did not stay to chat.

'Yes, please.' Her own voice, thin with shock.

'In your chair?'

'Yes.'

'There you are, dear. Eat up for your big day.'

Big day? She peered down on the tray. Boiled egg, a tiny glass of orange juice, a cup of greyish tea. Perhaps at some unremembered time, she had ticked a box agreeing that this would be her breakfast, every day; just as she had seemed to tick another box, permitting the world to call her by her Christian name.

'I am not Patricia, apart from to my dearest, oldest friends,' she thought. 'I am Mrs Avery, and I'll thank you to remember it.'

She did not say it. Instead: 'Thank you,' she murmured, as the pink shape backed out through the door. She would eat later, she thought. Instead, with the same habitual gesture, she lifted the mirror back before her face.

And what was that? A mass of movement, of childish arms and legs, hair of all shades blowing in the wind; herself in the middle, laughing, half winded by the mayhem of it all. Granny Pat: a role she had played to perfection. Memories of the day came back to her. A birthday perhaps, when all the family had come together, and she had made lunch – roast beef for everyone, that had been a strain – and then afterwards they had gone outside, to sit on the veranda. How grateful she had been to stretch out on a lounger, a glass of something in her hand. But the children had called for her, and she had gone to them, their fairy grandmother, to stand in their circle while they whooped and danced around her.

The grandchildren: how she had loved them. Girls, most of them, who loved sifting through her pretty things, the piles of beaded evening bags and scarves. Girls who had gazed, enraptured at photographs of her and Jack in evening dress; or her alone, on a beach, limbs oiled, like someone in a magazine. She put the mirror down. How close she had felt to those children, delighting in their confidences, trying not to laugh. Shining in their innocence and adoration. And now?

Now they did not come. Now no one came, and had not come for months. Not grandchildren, nor daughters, nor Jack – though Jack could not come, for he was not alive – nor anyone she had befriended in her long years of living in the town. Voices reached her from the corridor; not passing, as she expected, but pausing, as though the people they belonged to were huddled just outside.

The door swung open. A tall woman, clear plastic curved around her face. Not Julie, not Nisha. Not a regular at all, she realized, but Mrs Garside, who had barely stepped into her room since the day she had arrived. Mrs Garside, manager of the home, shaking her head a little at the untouched tray. 'Eat up, Mrs Avery. It's not every day that you make history.' What history do you mean, she tried to ask; but had not time to say it, before the looming figure swished out through the door.

As it shut, she saw Jack's face; reflecting from the paintwork. Jack, looking out at her, holding their new-born child. Linda: so sweet and soft. 'Linda': the name that she had chosen. Beautiful, it meant, and beautiful the child had been, though strangely she had never cared. She had grown up tall and gangly, bookish, smitten with her father; not the daughter she had hoped for, to help her in the house. After that had come Diana, the hunter. Diana had been the one she had cleaved to most: wiry and determined, with hair as tight-curled as her own. And finally, Rosemary, for remembrance, the girl they had not wanted to grow up. No boy, of course. And that had been a problem, for Jack would have liked a boy. He was working hard by then, building up the business, closed off in his workshop. Injection moulding, a process she did not understand. Plastic shapes, whose use she did not know. A boy could have learnt all that, but not a girl. That they had agreed on. The girls had gone off to the convent for their schooling, then to Switzerland. And then they had come back, to marry in their turn.

She had felt lucky to have girls, and yet in different ways they had rejected her. Linda, the eldest, most of all. Linda, who never seemed to bother how she looked. Linda, who had met a man they knew was trouble and – though Patricia had warned her against him - had married him nonetheless, bringing trouble to them all. Mistakes that had been made.

'Come along now, Mrs A. Oh, you do look nice today. All ready for your big day?'

More voices, bodies, jostling into her room. Kind, practised hands – the sort that did not take resistance - loading her into a wheelchair. Then out into the corridor, walls and pictures rushing past. The shush of wheels on carpet. Doors parting. Stop! Where are we going? A laugh above her head. 'Just a little drive. You're a part of history, Mrs A.'

Moving, gazing out; another scene appearing in her head. Her own mother, sitting weeping. A silent weeping that continued, unrelenting, as each exercise book was examined, corrected, and laid upon the pile. Her brother, Henry stretched out, fiddling with his stamps. She herself, standing by, aghast. Their father dead – dead by then at least a decade; their mother's great grief still unquenched. Back working as a school teacher, now she was a widow. Always busy, always tired. Henry older, cutting himself off. And she herself, so lovely, so desirable – she saw it daily in men's faces – and yet unsure. What could she do with herself? Not clever, particularly, but full of life. Full of laughter and fun and a terrible giggling silliness that spilled over with her friends. A laughter and a silliness she could not show at home.

How to get out of there? It was not much later that men began to hang around; men from the church and other places, men who were unmarried or simply could not stop themselves. Younger men too, whom she did not know or trust. And Jack – John, as she had called him then. Serious. Thoughtful. Brown wavy hair, a touch receding. A pleasant, gentle face. He took her in a punt along the Thames, while she gazed up at him, her mother decorous in the prow. And then she had married him, in a dress that was mauve, not white. A choice she had regretted afterwards, and only proved that she was foolish. Her brother frowning as he led her down the aisle.

'We're here now, Mrs A.'

More hands, ladling her out, out of the van or ambulance, out into the cold. Then in through spreading doors, along a corridor, wide and empty, smelling of disinfectant. A place that could only be a hospital. She took a breath. The world beyond seemed distant now. A strangeness in her chest, as though a fly or moth had stolen into it and fluttered in the space between her ribs. Here for some scan or other, for some worn-out part of her she had forgotten. When she looked up next, a face was poised above her. Handsome, she could see that clearly, with eyes that shimmered with feeling and concern. Eyes that were blue, above a mask of paler blue: the colour of...speedwell, that was it, the spreading plant that had threaded though the lawn of their first house. Jack. Her dry lips parted. He had come for her at last.

'Just a sharp scratch, Mrs Avery.'

He was strangely dressed, she saw, in sheets of crinkling plastic, not like Jack at all. She sought instead the blueness of his eyes, thirsting for it, more strongly than for any drink. Eyes that, as he pushed the needle into her, seemed suddenly to well with tears.

'Don't cry, Jack,' she found herself saying. Then, as the eyes shone brighter. 'It will be all right.'

He stared back, tender, acknowledging their private truth. Too soon, he sat back, the bliss of their togetherness already past. A swab of cotton pushed against her mottled skin.

'Keep well, Mrs Avery.'

Her chair was gripped and propelled away. She protested, wishing to stay longer with the man who looked like Jack, and perhaps had even been him; a thing she would have known for certain if they had only let her stay. But what was this? People standing, in the corridor that before had been empty. Standing, waiting, raising their arms as though in greeting. Men and women, some in uniform – nurses, surely, and doctors too – tired eyes smiling above their masks, lifting their hands as she approached and clapping. Clapping? Surely not clapping her? And yet it seemed they were. Clapping, yes, and cheering, and pointing cameras, or so it seemed, by the bright lights flashing in her eyes. People who wished her well. People who loved her – yes, she did not imagine it, love shone in their eyes, and tears, that were mixing with that love, combining with the clapping that did not die away as she drew close, but built to a crescendo.

'History', the word was whispered as she passed. Somehow, they knew her for who she really was. Not old Mrs A, mind fraying, forgetful and forgotten; but Patricia Avery, dazzling, mesmerising, the star she should have been.

Patricia Avery: the first to get the vaccine. First in the hospital, the town, the county: it did not matter which. First, for all she knew, in the country or the world. Patricia Avery, a name synonymous with hope. Patricia Avery who, when the microphone is thrust towards her, can say, to these people who look like Jack and Linda, and Rosemary and Diana, and Henry and her mother – and there, over there, surely she can see her father; can say, with the wisdom that comes over a life-time: 'Please, do not worry. Things will get better. Everything will be all right.'

Jag Älskar Dig, Auntie
by Hanna Järvbäck

This suitcase of mine
Is far too heavy.
It overflows
With the things she left me.
And not a single thing did I want to miss.

Scattered on the bottom you will find,
Jewellery she kept close and always mixed.
Silvers and golds.
If that is not bravery,
Then I don't know what is.

Jammed in the corner are her glasses,
To help me see.
Because one day she told me,
That despite my eyes are green,
I watch and judge with blue,
And that would make it harder to start anew.

In the middle I have wrapped
The things she told me to care for, gently.
Like the left eye teardrops from her sister,
And the blood from the heartbreak of her mother.
The disorientated mind of her husband,
And the very memory of her soul.

And the suitcase is overloaded,
With all the words,
They all had to say.
Of all the advice she always gave.
To never ropa "hej" förrän du är över ån,

And always kolla till bordet,
När du sparkat med tån.

In this suitcase of mine,
I have put in her shoes,
Although in them I will never walk.
And I cried when I packed her last words,

Jag älskar dig,
And goodbye.

Heritage

by Emma Ormond

I have inherited your cosmic purple carrots,
hollow crown parsnips
and bleu solaise leeks.
I pull them from your garden
on the day of your funeral,
fearful that Mrs Davis down the street
will harvest them in the night
I can't let people take parts of you
even though I've said goodbye to your body.

At home my muddy haul
stains tablecloth and worktops,.
I begin to clean and cut
blackcurrant coins of carrots,
sandalwood chunks of parsnip,
oil, sea salt and under the grill
where they soften
the lump still in my throat.

I toast our last meal with red wine,
taste comfort in roots,
that have spent more time with you
than I have lately.
Imagine you laughing at the vicar's face
when I told him there would be no headstone
and planted Glaskins Perpetual Rhubarb on your grave.

Absent Ghost
by Amy James

The house felt so empty. That was my first thought on walking through the door. It smelt wrong somehow, the dead air and undisturbed dust combining to make it feel abandoned. The energy was different as well - there was something missing, something changed, just something off. It was dim. The sky outside was grey, despite the promises of the weather forecast, it definitely looked like it was going to rain. The clouds had gathered in an oppressive manner, and despite it being midday in June, the place was a mass of shadows. Half-familiar shapes gathered in dark recesses; under the stairs, around the corner, and the portraits on the walls recalled earlier days. They showed happy, smiling, younger faces, not yet strained by pressure; or fear, or loss. God,it felt strange in here.

My brother had come here the week before, to help tidy the garden. He had always been the rational, collected one, had held himself together far more admirably than I ever could. But he had only been able to spend a couple of minutes in the house before he couldn't stand it anymore. He had told me afterwards that he felt he had to get out. In the end, he spent most of the visit sitting outside in the car, anxious to leave. My brave, strong little brother.

I was desperately trying to tell myself I had to be brave. For Nan, for Dad. For myself. I could feel the lump in my throat hardening with every swallow, threatening to choke me, and the prickling feeling in my nose and eyes wouldn't leave. My Dad came up behind me with a box, and I unwillingly moved further into the house, looking around, my skin crawling as I half expected some sign of life. So often I had walked in and all had seemed still for a second, before her head would pop around the kitchen door, and

I would breathe a sigh of relief. For the last few years of her life, every time we came to visit I had been irrationally terrified of finding her dead. But I should have known she wasn't. It had never felt like this before.

Still, her very presence was in every aspect of the house, like fingerprints on the glass of a window. Everything sang to me. The chair she used to sit in for brief periods of time, before inevitably finding the next thing that needed doing. The way her knitting bag still rested against the wall, as though waiting for her arthritic, but still clever, fingers to pick up their work once again. The metal tin, always full of biscuits that I could never quite resist. It hadn't felt quite the same when my Grandad had died a few years before. This was their place, a plot of land that they had been gifted for their wedding over 60 years before, a house that had been created just for them. Furnishings made by my Nan, metalwork created by my Grandad. A garden bursting with flowers, topped with a vegetable garden and the old, crabbed, apple tree where his ashes were scattered - where one day soon, both of their ashes would be scattered. They had built this place together, made something of a bare patch of ground. It had always felt so solid, so permanent, as much as my grandparents had. Until they suddenly weren't. When he had died, she was still there, the spirit of them both was still there. But now, this place which had always felt integral to my family, more even than my own home, changed. It felt empty, and yet it felt haunted.

Haunted by memories of a lifetime of Saturday afternoons while Dad was at the football, and summer holidays playing with toys in the garden. Days when it tipped down and I breathed against the glass of the French door facing the garden. Curling up with a book when anxiety threatened to overwhelm me. Sitting in the grass, making 'perfume' with flowers and fairy liquid. A moment of fear when my Grandad lost his temper, not realizing until years later that it was fear of his encroaching dementia that made him do so. Watching my Nan cook, apron tight around her waist. The taste of coconut cake on a Sunday with my family around and my brother trying to eat as much chocolate as possible unnoticed. The cardigans she knitted, the smell of his raspberries in summer, the notes on the side, the photos from their 60th wedding anniversary. All there, haunting a house that she was forever gone from. In such a space, a place she had always been so much a part of, her lack was almost more noticeable than she had been while there. Present by her very absence.

KEEPER OF WALKS

Keeper of Walks
by Gail Mosley

Let's just say I'll miss the long-legged stride,
single file or alongside,
me on the right for the good ear,
walking, talking, listening,
or, like as not, easy with quiet.

Stopping to breathe.
Noticing treecreeper, robin, red kite,
a familiar flower, name, forgotten, found
in the rain-speckled wildflower book.

Searching out lunchtime perches,
riverbanks, tree stumps, walls, boulders,
bird hides,
sheltered churchyard benches.

Puzzling over maps
for the path, barn, field corner,
ready to retrace steps,
down here, yes, back on track.
Owning every walk.

I am the keeper now.

AN UNEXPECTED MEETING IN 2020

An Unexpected Meeting in 2020

by Judi Moore

I heard her cough before I saw her –
that cough distinctive as a pheasant's call.
Suddenly, after the rain had stopped
and I went out, alone, into the orchard,
she was there with me among the apple trees
up to her knees in mist. Now she stepped into focus.
"You conjured me," she said, "with all your talk
of yellow flowers and sadness, and the clearing up shower."
I had quite forgotten how I towered over her
in later years. Her widow's hump made her
into a bun of a woman, almost as round as she was tall.
(And she was fond of a saffron bun.)

"Hello Mum," I said. "Today feels like your birthday."
"No, it's not. I'm dead not daft you know, m'dear."
"I feel it is, here in my heart. We've had
a strange year. I miss you more than ever."
"I know," she said. "I broke your brolly
in the rain today, Mum. Sorry." "You kept
that cheap old thing for nearly thirty years?
It was old when I died." "I know. But it was yours.
The one you sneaked the cuttings into
ambling round the gardens of the National Trust."
I heard her wheezy chuckle. "You and dad never had
a lot of stuff. We kept what there was to keep."
"I hope you keep me in your heart?" "Yes, always there."

I felt her breath – the softest touch of lips –
upon my cheek, just like the goodnight kiss

AN UNEXPECTED MEETING IN 2020

I'd get when I was six.
And she was gone.

Inu Irin Ajo
by Tinu Ogunkanmi

Fired. They'd fired her. Melody still couldn't believe it as she stood there waiting on the platform. Her train had been delayed for the last 20 minutes. Something about an accident close by was all she could make out from the flurry of information that was passing through her head at a staggering speed. She was, strangely, neither here nor there. Like she was floating elsewhere and not at all standing on that Overground platform, supposedly on her way to Tia's engagement dinner.

She didn't know whether to laugh or cry but she knew her composure must be kept because 'one couldn't cry in a public place', that's what her sister had taught her. 'As black women,' she would start by saying, 'we have to behave in a certain way.' At this point in her spiel, Sarah would look Mel straight in the eyes so Mel knew she meant business. In return, Mel would internally roll her eyes. She had never really been fond of that ideology.

Music was playing through her earbuds, but she wasn't paying attention to it. *Focus Mel, FOCUS!* She couldn't keep her thoughts in order at all. She pleaded with herself, shutting her eyes tightly in an attempt to hold back the tears threatening to make an appearance. After a few beats, when she felt as though she'd successfully tightened the bolt on the cage that held her tears, she opened her eyes and let out what would be the first of many sighs to come. She hated that she knew what was coming. The questions, the faces of pity, and the I-Told-You-Sos lingering like an unrelenting cold. She thought of the faux smile she'd have to plaster on her face for the whole night and visibly grimaced.

Why me? Mel asked herself. When she had dropped out of university five years ago, panic had set in like a wave,

142

unable to settle. She hadn't known what to do next. And now here it was again – the panic – enveloping her in a stronghold, slowly increasing its pressure on her neck, her breath quickening, and her anxiety in complete disarray. *Bro, what am I gonna do now? Nah, but how am I gonna pay my BILLS?* The voices swirling around in her head were getting louder and louder to the point that she hadn't heard her train finally approaching. A step too late it seemed; she'd missed her train.

'Fuck!' She groaned, instinctively bringing her arms to rest on her head. As if her day couldn't get any worse, Mel was officially late for the dinner. Tia was going to kill her. In fact, on her tombstone, it would read *Melody Ibukunoluwa Ayodele: 1994-2019. Unfortunately, but not shockingly, slain by a close friend.*

It was all jokes of course but everyone knew Tia's penchant for being on time (which didn't bode well with her already bad temper) and everyone knew that Mel was always late. Mel couldn't help it though. The African timing she'd grown accustomed to all her life meant that it was almost second nature to her, turning up late to events. Mel revelled in the gush of warm wind brought by the appearance of another train. She stood on the train; her body pressed against the glass panel adjacent to the train doors. Just a few feet ahead of her, Mel spotted a family of three in the middle seating aisle huddled together.

The mother was in the middle while her two children leaned on her from each side. They held onto her tightly as they tried to sleep through the monotonous whizzing of the train. Mel felt a sudden pang of jealousy shoot through her. The minutes passed by quickly with Mel staring at the heart-warming scene in front of her. Before she knew it, Mel and her numb feet were climbing up the escalator and out of Canada Water. She sighed again and tried to orient herself to her new surroundings. Significant time had passed; the clouds were tinted pink as the opening act for the sunset, reflecting beautifully on the legions of stunning high-rise apartments circling the Thames.

Spotting the nearest crossing, she strolled towards it and waited there for the man to turn neon green in its black box. At this moment, she found herself again trapped by her thoughts. This time, however, she pondered on her identity and why she always felt like an unwelcome visitor in her own body. You see, this happened quite a lot when Melody was feeling down. She could confess only to herself in the unfavourable dark of the night that she simply hated herself. It didn't help that all the people around her were in such great positions in their lives – her sister Sarah was a big-time banker in Canary Wharf, Lara was getting promoted, Tia was getting married, and her dad was madly in love with his new girlfriend, Agnes. All so happy and content in their personal and professional lives. But where was Mel? They all knew who they were... But who was Melody Ayodele?

Maybe I should just turn back. It was still a half-hour walk to the venue, situated in Surrey Quays. Maybe she'd say she was physically ill or nauseous (they didn't have to know *right away* that she had been fired). As if they'd a mind of their own, Mel could feel her feet taking steps forward.

At least Mel could say the weather was lovely. There was a nice easy breeze in the air. Soft, with a comfortable level of heat – but that was because of the unrelenting rain from the past two days. She took in the myriad of lofty trees lining the path, the smell of their rough bark, and how sturdy they appeared. They were where they belonged. She admired that about trees. Mel ambled like that for over 15minutes, admiring the trees and wallowing in her own sadness, until she came to a zebra crossing. She couldn't hear the loud beep of the sleek SUV honking at her over the noise of her thoughts as she took those two steps forward. The vehicle collided with her body, sending her high into the air before bringing her back down violently to the hard gravel of the road.

Opening her eyes felt like a sensation Mel had never experienced before. Everything felt alien, and that filled her with complete dread and a new surge of anxiety. A swarm of people sped past her at lightning speed, pushing a table with a figure atop it through white double doors. Then came the voices and the shouting and the wailing. Mel took hesitant steps in the direction of these sounds, curious as to where they were coming from, before she was in complete view of her father, Sarah and Lara all sat down. Sarah was holding Lara, silently trying to console the hysterical cries coming from her. Her dad, Timothy, stared in the direction of the double doors with an expression she'd only seen once before – at her mother's funeral. His face was bleak but so totally indifferent at the same time. Timothy couldn't look away, not this time.

'Daddy, what's going on? You're scaring me. ANSWER ME, PLEASE!' Mel screamed. She waved her hands to try and get their attention, but nothing worked; she couldn't believe that they couldn't see her. *That's not possible!* She thought as she turned away from them to slowly wander in the direction of those doors. Melody regretted it almost immediately, as her eyes came to focus on the scene in front of her. There lay her almost lifeless body, eyes shut while two doctors and a number of nurses worked all over her. The gasp she let out sent her to her knees and she couldn't breathe. How was she here but also there? She closed her eyes and opened them again, repeating the process several times as if that would change what she was seeing. It didn't. *It's just not possible! Why me? It's always me!*

She didn't realize that she'd stood up and marched out of the room; her vision was blurry from the tears cascading down her face. Mel certainly didn't realize that a force, unrecognisable to her, was pulling her in the direction of a new set of doors – she was focused on the fact that she was dying, you see. The crying and the scattered voices of medical workers were all too much for her. So loud and so intense, her head throbbed trying to block them out.

Something beckoned to her. She suddenly felt a flurry of warmth come over her, a thump in her heart, so heavy like rocks. Looking up at the doors stood just a few feet before her, with a bright light coming through from behind it, she felt compelled to go through them. Maybe here, she'd get the relief she so desperately wanted. *It cannot be any worse than this.* With a flash from the blindingly white bright light, Melody found herself in a place that was definitely not the hospital.

'Wow!' She whispered, in utter shock at the sight she was viewing. In lieu of a blue sky was a remarkable celestial sky. It was completely ethereal, with amethysts and amaranths and azures all mingling in wonderful harmony.

As she walked the length of the long road, dusty and saffron in colour, Mel couldn't help asking, 'Am I bugging or is this Nigeria?' There was a line of lived-in huts with thatched roofs lining her pathway, but the weather was the biggest indicator. It was sweltering and biting in the way she remembered her dad had described to her.

'Why am I wearing *iro** and *buba**?' Melody asked herself, looking down at herself in bewilderment. She was no longer in her earlier ensemble of a white shirt, black trousers and heels. No, the *iro* and *buba* she wore instead were persimmon orange and paired with matching flip-flops.

Mel soon found something else to focus her attention on. She followed the aroma of spices that wafted by her nose and wandered onto a compound. Here on this compound, Melody was met with a long path. On each side of this dusty path were palm-fronted market stalls adorned with an array of food and accessories. She saw luminous figures – *ghosts* – of women, dressed in black *iro* and *buba*, sitting and loudly bantering while preparing food. Mel noticed that they all spoke her mother-tongue, Yoruba. She smiled as she walked past them. It all seemed so familiar and homely. She loved their fondness of each other. Their attire and their gossip. For the first time in a very long time,

Melody felt like a tree.

All so suddenly, the concurrent sounds of the chatter and laughter seemed to fade away. Just by blinking, Mel found herself at a park with a swing at its centre and other recreational apparatus scattered to the side. It was still the same dusty saffron-coloured roads, and still the same star-spangled sky. In front of her stood a familiar figure. Mel gasped when she registered who it was.

'*Aaro re nso mi**, my child.' The figure said and took a step forward, stretching out her hands to envelop Melody in an embrace. *I've missed you.* Melody stepped back, unwilling to feel the array of emotions bursting at the seams. It was her mother, Sade. She was clothed in a mix of black and royal blue *iro* and *buba* of the finest silk and chiffon. She was a slender woman, whose frown lines had deepened on her smooth cocoa skin over the years due to hard work as an underpaid nurse. In photos Mel had seen, Sade always looked perpetually tired, but here, as she stood tall and grand in front of Mel, she seemed brighter – even brighter than the other luminous figures she'd seen.

'What? You can't greet your own mother in death after 20 whole years?' Sade spoke, with her beautiful gap-toothed smile that her father loved so much.

'You left me behind... and now you're here? Why? How?' Mel asked as she violently shook her head. The throbbing had returned in the tenth fold.

The park felt so serene at that moment. The large red swing set was still, as if frozen entirely. The ground looked a bit darker than it had moments ago but maybe it was Melody's imagination. All that could be heard was Mel's unsteady breathing. Before speaking, Sade paused to take a deep breath.

'You know something, Ibukun?' She started by saying, 'When I first started my journey here, I begged and *begged* to go back. I needed more time with you, with your sister, with... my love. My sweet soulmate. I watched you all every day go through the hard times.' Remorse was etched clear as day on her face. 'I wanted to hold you and tell you that it was okay in those times you were alone... That you felt so alone... broke me inside all over again.' Sade took a break, tears pooling at the corner of her eyelids.

'You see Ibukun, you need to stop pushing people away and let yourself heal. You are not alone, my sweet child. My death does not mean that I am gone. No, I am with you *always*. If I could have stayed, you know I would be right there *always* holding your hand... guiding you... loving you.' Mel could no longer stand the distance between them.

She leapt into her mother's arms, hugging her so fiercely at that moment, sobbing with her knees weak, completely broken.

They stayed like that for a while with Sade holding her, comforting her the way Mel had always craved for years until the last mews coming from Mel came to a slow stop. Sade took her hand and led her to one of the engine-red swing seats and plopped her down firmly. Sade began to push her, and at first, Mel found it so silly, but she started to grin wide like a Cheshire cat. They played and talked like that for a while. Sade told Mel all about her childhood and how difficult it was moving to a new country where she never felt appreciated.

'I loved the thought of education and I wanted to be more than just a wife, you know. What opportunities were there in Nigeria for a woman like me? Your father and I, oh my... we struggled for years to scrape up the money to come to Britain. We didn't want you girls to go through what we had to... but it wasn't easy when we finally *did* leave.' They shared looks of understanding and cried together.

After more time passed, Sade took Mel's hand again and silently walked with her for a while, until they came to a fork in the road. Sade reluctantly let go of Mel's hand and went to go stand on the left side. As soon as Sade got there, more luminous figures appeared. They seemed so familiar to Melody and she felt warm just being in their presence. They were all women, dressed in black and blue like her mother, standing in an arched row looking at her, smiling fondly. This was her family; her people. And she was their legacy. Melody knew then that she couldn't stay. No, she *had* to go back; make amends, and do better this time around. Her ears tingled in anticipation, but she was confident in her decision.

'Thank you,' Mel said. Not just to her mother, but to all the women that stood before her.

'Take care of my soulmate for me,' Sade called out to Mel. Salty tears started pooling at the corner of Mel's eyes. This time, Mel did not want to hurriedly wipe them away. She wanted to feel them roll down her cheeks and not have to hold in her emotions anymore. She mouthed 'I love you' to her mother as she walked right. She kept walking and walking until that blindingly bright light appeared again, obscuring her vision.

Lying down with her eyes closed on an uncomfortable hospital bed, with her father holding her hand in both of his while saying some silent prayers, a small smile crept onto Melody's face. A tree at last.

Glossary

Buba – a blouse
Aaro re nso mi – I've missed you.
Iro – a large piece of fabric worn wrapped around your lower half; like a skirt. The iro and buba are worn together.

Salty Eid
by Judith Allnatt

Rima pauses in the echoing stairwell of the London high-rise, her mop slowing to stillness as a smell of cooking reaches her nostrils: rich, meaty and riddled with spices. She sniffs, breathing in the fragrance of tender chicken, garlic, paprika and allspice. Shish Taouk. Although hunger fills her mouth with saliva, it is a different longing that overtakes her, speeding her heart. This is a scent she hasn't smelt for years - the smell of her Syrian home. She hauls the heavy bucket up to the fifth floor landing and dumps it down, heedless of the slopping water. She leans on her mop, a slight 15-year-old dressed in an over-large sweatshirt, holey jeans and trainers with no laces, her dark, curly hair stuck damply to her forehead.

Shish Taouk! Her eyes fill as she pictures her mother in the steamy kitchen of their apartment in Aleppo. She remembers her deft hands chopping herbs, sprinkling salt and all the time talking: 'Rima, how was school? Pass me the plates to warm. No, not the chipped ones: the ones with roses that your father likes. You think I make beautiful food to put it on ugly crockery?' Under her mother's voice is the sound of the TV from the other room where her little brother, Yusef, watches cartoons and from outside comes the sound of traffic and birds. It is like a breach in time, this glimpse of a long-gone day - before the coming of the Awfulness - so ordinary and yet so precious: the soundtrack from another world.

Her nostrils widen as she draws in more of the aroma that is coming from apartment 5C. Her stomach rumbles loudly. She's been surviving on one meal a day, spooning in baked beans or tuna straight from the tin. She draws nearer to the door. Legs like water, she leans against it and it gives under her weight. It opens onto a hallway where an old woman in a hijab is bending to stroke a tabby cat.

The old woman asks with mild curiosity, 'Who're you?'

Rima babbles, 'It was open! I wasn't doing anything, honestly! It was the smell, the smell of the food.'

The old lady looks her up and down and says to the cat, 'A visitor.' She takes Rima's arm. 'Come in, child, you look half-starved. Come, eat.'

***

As Rima wipes her plate with flatbread, soaking up every last drop of garlicky oil, the old woman, whose name is Yara Nassir, asks where she's come from and what brought her to London.

'Aleppo. We were supposed to find my uncle, Karim Terzi, here in Acton. You don't know him do you?'

Yara shakes her head. 'A lot of people here.'

'No one knows him,' Rima says dully. 'He isn't here.'

'Can't the resettlement people help you find a relative?'

Rima fidgets. 'He's not a real uncle; we just called him that. He's a friend of my parents.'

'Well, I could still help you. Take you down to Borough Hall to Citizen's Advice.'

Rima glances at the door.

'You have got papers?' Worry crosses Yara's lined face. She puts a hand on Rima's arm.

Rima freezes. She wants to run but feels it would be disrespectful to an elder and to the hospitality she's received. 'No papers.' She mutters it as if saying it quietly will make it of less consequence.

'So you came in by boat,' Yara says grimly. 'Tell me.'

Rima's body is strung tight as a wire. She's caught between the desire to tell someone, to loosen for a moment the grip of her memories, and the fear that it'll lead to trouble. She passes her fingernail to and fro across the plastic cloth on the table, contemplates the marks she scores on the patterned surface. Yara ducks her head to look into her face. Rima sees that her eyes are determined, kind.

'The city was a ruin. When there was no water left we had to leave,' she begins. She will tell it as a series of facts. That's the only way she can do this: chronological facts to impose order on the unthinkable. 'My father went to get what supplies he could. He was killed when a rocket hit the market. We still had to go. There was no water, you see?' She speaks in a monotone.

'We paid the men a lot of money, almost all we had. When we crossed to Greece the sea was rough. I thought we would all be drowned but somehow we made it. Then we travelled day and night. The truck stank. There was nothing to eat until the camp in France.' She struggles to keep her voice level. 'My brother, Yusef, had a fever but we had no medicine . . .'

Yara's bony hand tightens on her forearm, willing her on.

Rima takes a long breath. 'After he died, others fell ill. We had to get out. We crossed to the UK at night.' She swallows hard. 'They put us in separate boats.' She can feel she has begun to rock backwards and forwards and tries to stop. This is what happens every time she comes to this point in her memory. Her fingers clench and unclench as if trying to find something that is slipping through them.

She skips ahead and starts again. 'When I got to London, I lived on the streets. It was easy compared to the camp - so much food just thrown away - and safer, as long as you keep out of sight. Then one night a couple of months ago, I was sleeping in a doorway, just here,' she nods towards the window. 'In the morning the caretaker found me and said I could sleep in the basement if I would do her cleaning.' She affects a shrug. 'So here I am.'

Yara holds her gaze. She is not so easily distracted. 'You said "we", Rima. Who did you come with? Who was put in a separate boat?'

'My mother,' Rima says in a voice so low it's almost a

whisper. She pulls her arm away. Then she's up, running down the hallway, out past the mop and bucket. She thuds down flights of stairs, ignoring Yara's voice echoing in the stairwell, 'Don't run away! Come back! Let me help you!'

***

That night, Rima lies under her coat on the pile of boxes she's squashed into a flat layer of cardboard to protect her from the cold of the storeroom floor. She tries to keep from thinking by staring at the words on the labels of the cartons of bleach and polish around her, straining her eyes in the dim streetlight that comes from a slatted window high above. It's no good. She loses concentration; the memories come and she is back there, on the beach in France.

Her mother is screaming her name as the men drag them apart. All the young girls are shoved into one boat and the rest into another. They're given life jackets but the dinghy bucks in the waves and she holds on tight to the nylon ropes stretched over the grey rubber. There are too many people in the boat. The girl next to her clings onto her and Rima is afraid that if they go in the water the girl will pull her down. All the time they were in the camp, her mother told her: 'Keep clear of the men. Don't walk alone; keep your eyes down; never go with them; scream if anyone touches you.' Now two men are taking her away. She sees the other boat set off and start to gather speed. She can't help it; she stands up, calling for her mother. One of the men shouts in her face and pushes her to her knees.

At some point in the night the wind gets up. Clouds rush across the face of the moon and the waves rise. Some of the girls cry out; their voices like the cries of seabirds taken by the wind. Rima tries to think logically as her mother has always taught her. She checks over her lifejacket looking for the tab that she might need to pull, but there is none and on the breast of the jacket there is only a strip of red material sewn on where the whistle should be. She hunches over in the fake jacket and whimpers with fear as the wind grows steadily worse. A faint streak of pink on the horizon dimly reveals white horses racing in to the shore. The dinghy is buffeted on the choppy water like a nutshell. Headlights flash from the beach. There is no sign of the other boat.

Then a squall sends a wall of water that hits them side-on and the whole boat flips. She gasps at the cold shock. Then she's under, water filling her mouth, muffling her ears, stopping her breath. Something hard hits her face - someone's shoe as they kick out - and she tumbles in the freezing water, flailing to find which way is up. When she surfaces, she is far from the upturned boat. There are shapes around it, people clinging on as the waves dash it towards the sands. She can't get to it against the force of the current. She goes under and up again, strikes out and is knocked back, struggles in the grip of the ocean until it spits her out like seaweed on the shore. She lies there, choking, sand rough against her cheek.

The vehicle is a van. In the beams of its headlights she sees a bedraggled procession pass as the other girls are herded towards it. A man gets out and counts them into the back. There is an altercation between him and the man who piloted the boat, who points towards the sea and shrugs. She lies very still. All the men get in and the van drives away. When the sound of the engine dies away she crawls up the beach, into the sand dunes beyond, and sits soaked and shivering amongst the marram grass, watching the sun come up. She scans the slate mass of the sea for the lighter grey of the other dinghy.

After an hour, she staggers along at the edge of the line of dunes, still looking, bending into the wind. It could have beached further up, she tells herself: of course it could. She looks for hours but finds nothing. She feels numb with dread. She tries to remember where it was her mother was taking them. London. Acton. But she can remember no more of the address, is not sure if she ever knew it. At a car park for the beach, on the rough palings of a fence, there are gloves in a row, all odd, all different colours. She touches one in puzzlement then realizes they've all been lost. She can't hold simultaneously in her mind a world where people place a lost glove where it will be found and the world in which she exists.

In the grey coastal town the next day, at the newsstand by the station, she sees photographs of the beach with little tents upon it, fenced off with orange tape, and behind them the unmistakable shape of an upturned dinghy.

***

It is Shawal, the month of fasting, and Yara insists that Rima eat with her at sunset. They sit together each evening and Yara tells of her life in Damascus, long before the war began. When Yara speaks of the Old City, its mosques, gardens and souks, it brings back to Rima the Aleppo of her childhood: Yusef running and sliding on the polished marble at the Umayyad Mosque, the smell of roses and pine trees, her mother's hands pouring a glass of tea. Sometimes she speaks of such things and Yara's brow furrows in sympathy. She seems to understand that beneath these bright memories Rima's loneliness is a deep pool, and that although reminiscing is irresistible, it is like running your hand across a glittering surface when you are terrified of the fathomless darkness that lies below.

As Eid approaches, the end of fasting, Rima dwells on the family gatherings they once had for the celebration: the stories, gossip and laughter, the kitchen fragrant with smells of meat, onion and ghee: for mainly savoury dishes are traditionally prepared for Eid ul Adha, 'Salty Eid'. Cousins, aunts and uncles came laden with plates of stuffed vine leaves and falafel to share. Food means so much more than mere sustenance. One night she says shyly to Yara, 'For Eid, I would like to cook for you. I'd like to make Kibbeh Safarjaliyyeh that my mother used to make. It was a family tradition; she never missed a year.'

Yara nods. Her face is solemn. 'We will honour your
mother in this way.'

'Some of the ingredients might be hard to get though. I'll
need quince and fresh pomegranate juice as well as lamb,
parsley, bulgur wheat and walnuts.' Rima's face falls. 'And
where can I get Aleppo peppers to make paste? Mother
wouldn't think of making it with anything else – no stuff in
jars.'

Yara frowns but then brightens. 'There's only one
place you'll get them. The world and his wife will be there,
getting what they need for Eid, so go early. You need to go
to Shepherd's Bush market. The green stall called Al Halal
Foods. That's the place.'

***

On the first day of Eid, Rima sets off with her list, a bag
and the money Yara has given her. Rivers of people of all
nationalities pass between tightly-packed stalls that display
handbags, clothes, foodstuffs, bedding and toys. At a stall
selling world foods she hears Muslim families exchanging
Eid greetings but she presses on to find the stall that will
have everything she needs. It is only as she thinks she
must have missed it, and must search the whole market
again, that she finally spots above the throng a bright green
awning and the words 'Al Halal'. She hurries towards it.

There are many women gathered there with their
backs to her, busy fingering the watermelons and sniffing
the cheeses, a blur of multicoloured dresses and hijabs.
But there is only one woman who ties her hijab quite that
way, whose shoulders slope at just that angle, whose hand
held out to take her change. Rima would recognize her
anywhere. Then she is pushing her way through the crowd,
pulling her mother round to face her and her mother's
startled face crumples as she sees her. Then they are in
each other's arms. They weep and rock together. Her
mother says Rima's name over and over and Rima, her

head against her mother's shoulder, breathes in her smell: the scent of warm skin, lemons, honey, cinnamon. Home.

Author Biographies

Alice Fowler

Alice Fowler is a writer based in Guildford, Surrey. She
is drawn to writing about people on the edges of society.
Landscape and the natural world are other sources of
inspiration. Having worked for national newspapers,
mainly as a feature writer, she is used to writing 'to length'
and enjoys the economy and freedom to experiment that
the short story brings. Her short story 'The Race' won the
Dorothy Dunnett Society/Historical Writers' Association
Short Story Award in 2020.
Email: alice.fowler@hotmail.co.uk; Twitter: @alicefwrites

Alison Nuorto

Alison is an EFL Teacher from Bournemouth. Her poetry
is inspired by an eclectic mix of poets, including Carol
Ann Duffy, Ben Okri, Wendy Cope and her former English
Teacher, Dr Joanne Seldon. Alison's poetry has appeared
in a couple of anthologies and she also won a local poetry
competition, run by Yellow Buses. The brief was to write
a Valentine's Day poem, to be printed on Valentine's Day
cards and distributed to passengers.

Amy James

Amy is an English student at Bournemouth University
currently in her final year. She has a special interest in
women in mythology and loves fantasy novels. When she
isn't reading or writing, she loves cooking, making her

own clothes and singing. She hopes one day to work in publishing.

Belinda Weir

Belinda Weir is a writer and poet, originally from Scotland, now living in the North of England. She has published stories in the 'Northern Crime One' anthology, the Scholastic 'Short Stories for Children' anthology, and poems in Dust poetry magazine. She's also been longlisted for the 1000-word challenge competition in 2019, highly commended in the Poetry on the Lake competition in 2018 and shortlisted for the 'To Hull & Back' competition in 2019. Belinda blogs about systems, complexity, hedgehogs and foxes, and leadership, and has worked in and with the NHS for most of her career.

Ben Stevenson

Ben Stevenson is a student, blogger and qualified ski instructor. He was born in Uruguay but grew up living in the Isle of Man and Spain. This peripatetic upbringing influenced his love for foreign cultures, languages and travel.

Bruce Harris

Bruce Harris is a Devon-based author and poet who has been consistently successful in short fiction and poetry competitions since 2003. Bruce has published three collections of short fiction, First Flame 2013, Odds Against 2017, and The Guy Thing 2018, and three poetry collections, Raised Voices 2014, Kaleidoscope 2017 and The Huntington Hydra 2019. See further details at www. bruceleonardharris.com. His first novel, 'Howell Grange', was published by the Book Guild in October 2019, and a fifth short story collection, 'Fallen Angels', in aid of the Huntington's Disease Youth Organisation, is to be published by the Guild on January 28th 2021.

David Butler

David Butler's novel 'City of Dis' (New Island) was shortlisted for the Irish Novel of the Year, 2015. His second short story collection, Fugitive, is to be published by Arlen House later this year. His third poetry collection, Liffey Sequence, is also to be published in 2021 by Doire Press.

Eimear Arthur

Eimear Arthur is an architect and writer from Ireland. She is interested in the inner lives of people and in how we relate to each other.

Elizabeth M Castillo

Elizabeth M Castillo is a British-Mauritian poet, writer and language teacher who lives in Paris with her family. When not writing poetry about love, languages or motherhood, she can also be found working on her webcomic, podcast, or writing a variety of other things under a variety of pen names. She has work in or upcoming in Selcouth Station Press, Pollux Journal, Authylem Magazine, and others.

Emma Ormond

Emma Ormond is a poet from Cambridge, England. She holds a PhD in insect ecology and references to plants, invertebrates and animals feature heavily in her work. Her poems have appeared in three anthologies and she was a runner up in the inaugural Fenland Poet Laureate (2013) and Ealing Autumn Festival Poetry Competition (2014). Recently she has been writing with other writers remotely to produce new and challenging work.

Hanna Järvbäck

Hanna Järvbäck is an international undergraduate student at the University of Brighton studying English Literature and Creative Writing. Born in Sweden, Swedish is her first language, however, since youth, found herself moved by the English language. She started writing creatively in English at the age of 15 and often includes a style of hybridity in her writing by mixing languages when discussing culture.

Jess Fallon-Ford

I am a twenty-year-old writer from Kent, England with a keen interest in the human condition. Themes explored in my work therefore include grief, loss, indentity, love and relationships, separation, regret, memory, healing, trauma and mental health. My sources of inspiration come from my own unique experiences and individual growth as well as the rapidly changing nature of the world around me. I work with a wide range of techniques including metaphorical conceit and allegory, rhyme, rhythm and natural imagery.

Joe Bedford

Joe Bedford is a writer from Doncaster, UK. His short stories have been published widely, including in Litro, Structo and the Mechanics' Institute Review, and are available to read at joebedford.co.uk. Twitter: @ joebedford_uk

Judi Moore

Since 1997 Judi has lived on fresh air and steam. Her life since then has been steeped in writing – her own, tutoring, beta-reading and reviewing the work of others, and simply reading. She writes poetry, short and long fiction, and reviews. Since moving to Weymouth in 2016 Judi has been inspired by the natural world surrounding her in Dorset. She is exploring, interrogating, and documenting it enthusiastically through her poetry.

Judith Allnatt

Judith Allnatt writes poetry, short stories and novels. Her historical novels, the most recent of which is The Silk Factory, have been variously featured as a Radio 5 Live Book of the Month and shortlisted for the Portico Prize and the East Midlands Book Award. Short stories have featured in the Bridport Prize Anthology, the Commonwealth Short Story Awards, and on BBC Radio 4. Judith lectures widely and is a Royal Literary Fund Fellow.

Les Clarke

He played in rock bands, was a stand-up comedian and actor. Toured in a show he wrote that contained 26 original songs. He's sold everything from shoes to double-glazing, perfume to D.I.Y. been a builder, office manager; fully qualified Financial Advisor, trainee train driver, police officer, weighbridge operator, chauffeur, bin-man, stores technician, and a learning difficulties support worker in a

psychiatric hospital. He now writes and directs stage plays and musicals.
lesclarkeplays@live.co.uk

Penny Frances

PENNY FRANCES' short stories have been published in literary magazines, including Mslexia, The Interpreter's House and Dream Catcher, and online with Horizon Review, Fictive Dream and Toasted Cheese. She has a Writing MA from Sheffield Hallam University and is currently seeking publication of her novel. She lives with her husband in Sheffield and works as a Senior Customer Advisor for the Local Authority. She blogs at pennyfrances. wordpress.com.

Rachael Hill

Rachael is a twenty-seven-year-old creative writer originally from Gloucestershire, but who now lives in Manchester, and has fallen in love with the North of England. She is currently studying Creative Writing at Manchester Metropolitan University, and has recently had several poems accepted for publication. When not reading or writing (and lockdowns permitting!) Rachael enjoys rock climbing, hiking, and generally adventuring in the great outdoors. You can contact her at rachaelanna93@gmail. com.

Richard Hooton

Born and brought up in Mansfield, Nottinghamshire, Richard Hooton studied English Literature at the University of Wolverhampton before becoming a journalist and communications officer. He has had several short stories published and has been listed in various competitions, including winning contests run by Segora, Artificium Magazine, Audio Arcadia, Henshaw Press and the Charroux Prize for Short Fiction. Richard lives in Mossley, near Manchester. rhooton@btinternet.com

Richard Smith

Richard is currently studying part time for an MA in Creative Writing at Keele University. He has been writing for nearly ten years and his short stories and flash fiction have been published in various anthologies, including Bridport Prize 2020, Henshaw Three and the Aesthetica Creative Writing Annual. He is currently working on his first novel as part of his dissertation for his MA. diyrichie@hotmail.com

Rosie Cowan

Derry-born Rosie Cowan is a former Guardian Ireland and crime correspondent currently doing a PhD in criminal law at Queen's University Belfast. Her short story, Little Wren, was one of 10 prizewinners from 1,468 entries in the Fish international short story competition 2020 and is published in the Fish 2020 anthology. She recently completed a psychological thriller featuring a female crime reporter on a London-based national newspaper.

Thandi Sebe

German-South African Thandi Sebe grew up in Cape Town. After completing her schooling at the German School in Cape Town she returned to her city of birth Berlin, where she completed an English BA at the Humboldt University. Since 2015 she has been working as an actor and writer for film and theatre between her two home bases Cape Town and Berlin.

Vivian Oldaker

Vivian has always written stories.
Andersen Press published her Young Adult novel "The Killer's Daughter" in 2009. Since then, Vivian has written novels, short stories and plays but sadly none of these has been snapped up by a publisher. Several of her short plays have been performed in front of polite audiences in Salisbury, Plymouth and Frome. She continues to write, in the hope that someone will read and enjoy.

Wendy Sacks Jones

Wendy is a journalist and former BBC correspondent. She has an MA in creative writing from St Mary's University, Twickenham, and is currently working on her first novel. She is a board member of the writers' collective 26 (which runs projects in partnership with charities and other organisations) and has had short-form prose and fragments of poetry published by 26 online and in print. She also teaches English to newcomers to Britain.

Printed in Great Britain
by Amazon

70719377R00102